CONVINCING
DAVID

CONVINCING DAVID

•

Jane McBride Choate

AVALON BOOKS
THOMAS BOUREGY AND COMPANY, INC.
401 LAFAYETTE STREET
NEW YORK, NEW YORK 10003

PRINTED IN THE UNITED STATES OF AMERICA
ON ACID-FREE PAPER
BY HADDON CRAFTSMEN, BLOOMSBURG, PENNSYLVANIA

To my aunt Tina, who is always there
with an encouraging word.

Chapter One

"But Ralph *likes* your bubble bath," Travis said.

"He should," Jenny agreed. The last of a very expensive bubble bath—a gift from her parents—and Ralph got to use it. Life was definitely unfair. She blew a strand of hair from her face.

"The next time you want to give Ralph a bath, use plain old soap, okay?"

"Okay." Nine-year-old Travis was already scampering away, leaving Jenny to deal with one very wet, very perfumed dog.

As if reading her thoughts, Ralph shook himself vigorously, soaking her.

Jenny wiped the water from her face and looked down at her shirt, now splattered with Ralph's bathwater. After drying herself as best she could, she patted him dry. He wriggled from her grasp, but she held on until she'd blotted most of the water from his shaggy coat.

"Okay, it's outside for you."

Ralph plunked down beside her.

She gave him a friendly pat on his rump.

He didn't budge.

She pushed him gently.

He laid his head on her lap and licked her hand.

Finally, she started to drag him toward the door.

Ralph yelped pitifully and remained planted on his haunches.

After a few minutes of tussling with the seventy-five-pound dog, Jenny sank back and admitted defeat. "You win. Just don't let it get around."

Ralph licked her face. She hugged him to her. What was a little water anyway? She looked at the disaster that used to be her bathroom and sighed. Wet towels littered the floor; spilled bath oil glistened on the counters and sink; muddy paw prints decorated the bath mat.

Travis peeked around the corner. "Hey, Jenny, you're not mad, are you?"

"No, I'm not mad. Just wet."

He threw his arms around her neck and hugged her. She tickled him until they both collapsed in a fit of giggles. Ralph joined in, pinning Jenny to the floor.

"Get off me," she ordered and shoved the dog with all her might.

"I'm sorry I used your bubble bath," Travis said. "But Ralph got all dirty when we were playing soccer." At Jenny's questioning look, he added, "Ralph's the goalie."

August had dragged by with only an occasional respite from the heat. She knew the kids were bored, restless. Mentally, she counted the days until school started again. Only about a week or so left of summer vacation. Surely she'd make it. If only her sense of humor—not to mention her sanity—held out.

"Jenny," Mr. Ambrose called. "The new boarder's here."

"Oh, no. He can't be. It's only one. . . ." She checked her watch and found it was three o'clock.

She thought about changing her clothes and decided against it. He'd have to take her as she was. With Ralph right behind her, she ran down the stairs.

A tall man stood in the hallway, gray eyes narrowed thoughtfully.

She nudged Ralph out of the way, resisted the urge to smooth her still-damp curls, and stuck out her hand. "I'm Jenny Kirtpatrick."

Warm fingers curled around her own. "David Sherwood."

She watched as David kept a cautious distance from Ralph.

"What is that thing?" He sniffed. "Is it wearing perfume?"

Jenny smiled. "That's Ralph. Travis gave him a bubble bath."

"You give your dog a bubble bath?"

"Not all the time," Travis piped up. "Just when he needs it."

"He looks like he's half horse."

"Baby fat," Jenny whispered.

"That's one big baby," David said.

She bent to scratch Ralph behind the ears. "He's really friendly. You'll see."

David looked doubtful. Jenny couldn't blame him. Ralph took a little getting used to. Another of her strays, her sister, Tessa, had called him.

She took her time studying David. Dark brown hair,

cut short, emphasized gray eyes framed by a heavy fringe of sooty lashes. A gray suit and burgundy tie made him look every inch the financial consultant he was. A friend of Tessa's and her husband, Jack, David had come to Colorado for a vacation.

There was something—a hint of sadness—that drew her gaze back to his eyes. They weren't cold but hurt. She doubted he was even aware of the pain that shadowed them. He looked as though he needed to learn how to laugh. For a moment, she wondered if she might be the one to help him.

Just what you need, she silently jeered. *Another stray to take care of.* Tessa's long-standing accusation that Jenny collected strays stung. Only, Jenny didn't see it that way. She saw a man in pain.

"Finished?" he asked.

Caught staring, Jenny flushed and then smiled. "Yes."

"Do I pass?" David hadn't meant his question to be taken literally. But Jenny Kirtpatrick appeared to do so.

She tucked a strand of honey-blond hair behind her ear and cocked her head to one side, chocolate brown eyes sparking with mischief. "I don't know yet. I'll let you know when I do."

He was trying to adjust to the idea that he actually might not pass muster when another interruption claimed his attention.

"Jenny, someone's emitting bad vibrations." An older woman wandered into the room and directed an accusing glare at David.

"Mrs. Abernathy, this is David Sherwood. Are you having another séance?"

"Yes. But it's not going well." She gave David a distrustful glance.

David stared at the woman, swathed in a dozen or more scarves and sporting a purple, bejeweled turban on her head. What was she? Another boarder? He'd already counted two children and two senior citizens. How many people lived in this menagerie?

When his friends had suggested Jenny's boarding-house in the Colorado mountains as a quiet place where he might take a much-needed vacation, they hadn't mentioned that her home resembled a human version of Noah's ark. How was he supposed to rest in such a place?

Already, he was regretting the decision to take time off. He hadn't taken a vacation in five years. What was he supposed to do with himself?

"Mrs. Abernathy, why don't you go back to the kitchen and try contacting Mr. Abernathy again?" Jenny suggested. "I have a feeling the vibrations will be better this time."

"All right, dear. If you're sure you're all right."

"I'm sure."

The old lady threw another suspicious look at David before retreating into the kitchen.

"Is she for real?"

Until then, Jenny had been cordial, even friendly. Her smile vanished. "Mrs. Abernathy is a member of the family."

"I'm sorry. I didn't mean—"

"It's all right," Jenny said. "Mrs. Abernathy seems a little strange, but she's really a dear." The smile was back in her eyes. Why did he experience a sudden surge of relief?

"Your brother-in-law and sister did tell you why I'm here, didn't they?"

Jenny nodded. "They said you needed a rest."

"It's Sheila's birthday," Travis announced.

"Trevor, go get Mr. Ambrose and Mr. Zwiebel and tell them it's time for the party."

David frowned. "I thought his name was Travis."

"I'm Travis."

Another boy appeared. David looked from one to the other. "Twins?"

"Nah," Travis—or was it Trevor?—said. "We just look alike."

"That's enough, Trevor," Jenny said. "Where's Katie?"

"Who's Katie?" David wanted to know.

"She's right here," Mrs. Abernathy said, carrying a plump blond-haired baby.

David's head was starting to hurt. "If that's Katie, who's Sheila?"

Jenny grabbed his hand, and a shiver of sensation snaked up his arm. "You'll see. We were just about to celebrate when Travis decided to give Ralph a bath."

David let himself be dragged through the back door and herded to the barn along with the rest of the family. A party in the barn? He shook his head.

Stopping in front of a stall occupied by an aging mare, Jenny introduced the guest of honor. "Meet Sheila."

"You're holding a birthday party for a horse?"

Jenny turned a smile on him as she held out an apple and a carrot. "Who wants to feed Sheila?"

"I do," Trevor said.

"Me too," Travis seconded.

Jenny quartered the apple with a knife from her pocket and handed them each a piece.

Not certain whether to turn tail and run or stick it out, David watched as the boys took turns feeding the horse.

"I think Sheila's had enough," Jenny said when the mare turned her head away from the rest of the apple. "Let's go back to the house and cut the cake."

"All right!" Travis shouted. He slipped his hand inside David's.

Tentatively, David closed his own around the small hand. It felt strange, though not unpleasant. Travis turned his face up to David's. "You're nice."

"I am?" He felt an unfamiliar flood of warmth envelop him.

The small boy nodded emphatically. "You're not like the other boarders. 'Course, they're nice too. Just different."

"Oh? How's that?"

"You don't have hair in your nose. They do."

Jenny coughed.

David pursed his lips to hide a grin. "Well . . . thanks. I think."

"Travis, you'd better hurry," Jenny said. "The cake will be all gone if Trevor gets there first. Tell Mrs. Abernathy to save David a piece."

"That's not nec—" he began, but the little boy raced off, leaving Jenny and David alone. "Nicely done."

"Thanks. I've had a lot of practice."

"Just for the record, how old is Sheila?"

"I'm not sure. She was here when I bought the

house, and she was old then. Eighteen. Maybe nineteen.''

''When did you buy this place?''

''Four years ago.''

David looked around, noting the weathered barn, the house that needed a new coat of paint, the poor condition of the fences, automatically calculating profit and loss. ''It must take a lot of work to keep up.''

She nodded. ''A lot of work and even more money.'' Brown eyes laughed at him. ''You want to help me fix up the place?''

He caught himself before visibly flinching. He wouldn't know a screwdriver from a hammer. He was a numbers man.

Jenny's sister had said that Jenny was hopelessly enmeshed in debt due to her inability to say no to anyone who needed a place to stay, a handout, a loan. Taking in boarders was supposed to offset the expenses of running such a big house, but he wondered.

He understood about the children—they were foster children, and she probably received a stipend for each of them. He doubted it covered the barest expenses, though.

''How long have you known Jack and Tessa?'' she asked.

''A couple of years. Great people.''

''My brother-in-law, Jack, has all the personality of a soda cracker. And Tessa organizes her spices alphabetically.''

She said it as if that explained everything. David suppressed a smile. She had them pegged, all right.

Jack and Tessa Reynolds were friends of his, but he wasn't blind to their shortcomings.

He watched as the expression in her eyes softened. "But they're family. They love me, and I love them."

His next words were interrupted as a denim-clad blur dashed past him to clutch at Jenny's leg.

"Jenny! Jenny! Travis put boogers on me." Trevor burst into tears, his face screwed up in lines of righteous indignation. He covered his eyes with his hand but left space to see if he was getting the proper attention.

Another blur whirled by him to grab at Jenny's other leg.

"Travis, did you do that?" Jenny asked.

"Only after he called me a nerdhead."

"That doesn't matter. Apologize to Trevor."

"Sorry," Travis mumbled.

"Louder."

"Sorry." Travis glared at Trevor. "What about me? Don't I get 'pologized to?"

Jenny looked at Trevor, who jammed his fists into his pockets. "Trevor." Her voice held a warning.

"Sorry." He spit on a grubby hand before holding it out. "Shake on it?"

Travis hesitated before spitting on and extending his own equally grubby hand.

David watched the exchange, feeling as though he'd entered another dimension, one completely removed from his own sane world of numbers and balance sheets. Somehow, in a way he didn't fully understand, he felt left out.

"Beat you to the creek!" Trevor called.

David stared in bemusement as the two boys now

scampered off, their altercation apparently forgotten.

"Ms. Kirtpatrick, if we could—" David bit off an oath at yet another interruption.

"Jenny, the washer is rumbling again," Mrs. Abernathy called from the porch.

"Rats." Jenny flashed him an apologetic smile. "Excuse me for a sec."

She ran to the house.

He followed at a slower pace. *A sec?* What kind of grown woman used words like "a sec"?

It appeared those weren't the only words Jenny knew. He struggled to catch the words that drifted through the open door as he climbed the porch steps.

"Great galloping gorillas." There was a loud thump.

"Hopping horseflies."

He cocked his head. *Great galloping gorillas?*

He started to get interested.

"Jumping jackals. Leaping lizards."

The lady seemed to be going through the whole animal kingdom, one letter at a time.

Cautiously, he pushed open the kitchen door. A green monster advanced toward him. "What the heck—"

"Save yourself," Jenny said. The grimace on her face told him she was only half joking.

He winced as his Italian loafers squished through several inches of water, but he didn't retreat. No matter what, he couldn't let her face the runaway washer by herself. If only he could get behind it . . . He reached for the plug, barely avoiding getting his toes squashed, and jerked. The washer hiccupped its way to an uneasy silence.

"Thanks," Jenny said. "I thought it was going to get me this time for sure."

"This time? You mean it's done this before?" He readjusted his necktie.

"Yeah." She shrugged. "It acts up about once a month or so. This was the worst, though."

"What do you intend to do about it?"

She looked surprised. "Wait till it's cooled down and then finish the laundry."

"You can't mean you're going to use it again?"

"I have to." She smiled. "Its bark's worse than its bite. Once it's rested, it'll be fine."

The feeling of having stepped into another dimension returned. "Washing machines don't need to rest. Not normal washing machines, that is."

She rewarded him with another one of those smiles that turned him inside out. "This isn't a normal washing machine. It's one of a kind."

"Thank heaven."

"They don't make them like this anymore," she said, patting the machine fondly.

"They haven't made them like this in the last fifty years," David said, eyeing the green beast warily. "It belongs in a museum. The Smithsonian would probably pay good money to put it in their Early Americana exhibit."

"Well, they can't have it until I finish my laundry."

"Jenny, what if something happens?" he asked, his forehead creased with worry.

"Like what?"

"Like the thing blows up and hurts someone."

Her smile was unconcerned. "I'm the only one who

uses it. Besides, it won't blow up. It just likes to spit and sputter to let me know who's boss.''

Her lack of concern for her safety made him angry. ''All the more reason to replace it.''

She began pushing the machine back against the wall. With a muttered oath, David set her aside none too gently and finished the job.

''Look, David, I appreciate your help, but I can take care of it. I've been doing it for a long time.''

He shoved a hand through his hair, his temper hanging by a fine thread.

''Well, since you're here, why don't I show you to your room?'' Jenny said as she started toward the stairs.

''Wait.''

She turned to look at him expectantly.

He wiped his brow. This wasn't going the way he expected.

Guileless brown eyes met his with an inquiring gaze. ''Is something wrong?''

He shook his head, unable to answer. The lady was a witch and had put him under a spell. That was the only answer. There was no other logical reason why he had spent the last fifteen minutes wrestling with an antiquated washing machine and then feeling he should apologize for maligning it. David believed in logic. Without it, where would the world be?

He started toward her, then stopped as his shoes squeaked. He looked down at them and wondered if disarming a renegade washing machine fell under the category of hazard pay.

''I am a little tired,'' he said and realized it was true. He *was* tired. But not from lack of sleep. He felt as if he'd just stepped through the looking glass.

"You'll feel better when you've had a rest. The mountain air affects a lot of people that way."

He grabbed at the explanation as a drowning man grasps at a life preserver. Mountain air. Of course. He was suffering from a lack of oxygen. Colorado wasn't called the Mile-High State for nothing. Memory of a visit to Chile niggled at him. He hadn't been affected by a lack of oxygen there. And the altitude had been several thousand feet higher.

"Uh . . . I'll see you in a couple of hours," he said, anxious to put some distance between himself and the disturbing woman who looked at him with eyes the color of a Hershey's chocolate bar.

She patted his arm. "I'll bring you some tea."

Tea? He frowned, trying to remember when he'd last had tea. "I don't want to put you to any trouble."

"It's no trouble," she said, her hand still resting on his arm.

He wanted to put his hand over hers to maintain the contact but resisted the urge. More bemused than ever, David started toward the stairs.

"Third door on the left," Jenny called over her shoulder.

"What . . . oh . . . thanks."

In the old-fashioned bedroom, he found a four-poster bed with a crocheted coverlet. Gingerly, he tested the mattress and found it incredibly soft. He sank back onto it, intending to sort out his thoughts for a moment.

A whiff of lavender teased his nostrils just before he drifted into a dream-filled sleep, where a green monster threatened to devour him. A slight figure with blond hair and brown eyes stood fearlessly between him and the monster, holding a plate of chocolate cake and a cup of tea. He couldn't make out her features. But she smelled faintly of lavender.

Jenny found him there. She set the tea on the nightstand. He looked much less formidable now with sleep softening the lines around his eyes and mouth. His hair, mussed from sleep, curled slightly across his temples.

She tiptoed from the room. David Sherwood wasn't what she expected. He puzzled her. And the hint of sadness in his eyes worried her. David looked like life hadn't given him much reason to smile.

Her lips curved upward. Maybe, with the help of the children and the others, she could change that.

The chemistry she'd felt between them when he touched her worried her. She didn't want to feel breathless around him, to go all weak kneed and tingly. The last thing she needed in her life was a man. Especially a self-proclaimed numbers man.

Whatever had happened between them was simply a chemical reaction, she reassured herself. She wondered why she had such a hard time believing it.

Chapter Two

"Jenny. Jenny, is that you?"

"Yes, Tessa, it's me." Jenny managed to keep the impatience from her voice as she cradled the phone between her chin and shoulder.

"What do you think of your new boarder?"

"He seems very nice," Jenny said, realizing it was true. "A little on the serious side."

"How're you doing? You know, about . . . money?" Tessa added the last word in a whisper, as though talking about such things was in poor taste.

"We're doing fine." Jenny crossed her fingers behind her back as she'd done as a child, hoping to negate the lie.

"I'm so glad. I feel a lot better now that I've talked with you."

"I wish I did," Jenny muttered under her breath and was again ashamed of herself.

"Did you say something?"

Desperately, Jenny tried to change the subject. "No. Now, tell me what the baby's been up to."

15

Tessa spent the next half hour relating the precious things Jack, Jr., had done. Jenny privately thought that Jack, Jr., sounded like a one-baby demolition team.

"He must keep you busy," she said, considering that the understatement of the year.

Tessa laughed. "You can say that again. But we love him to pieces. I've never been so happy. That's why I want you to find someone, settle down, and have babies of your own." The last word came as a quick gasp. "I'm sorry, Jenny. I didn't mean—"

"It's all right." Jenny drew a sharp breath and reminded herself that Tessa loved her and only wanted her sister to be as happy as she was. "I have three children now. Just because they're not my biological children doesn't mean I don't love them."

"Of course you do," Tessa said. "But they're still *other people's* children. It's not the same as if you'd adopted them." When Jenny didn't reply, Tessa pressed, "Well, is it?"

"I've got to go now, Tessa." Jenny didn't bother to cross her fingers behind her back this time. Sometimes a lie was necessary. This was definitely one of those times. "Someone's calling for me." She hung up before she could say something she'd regret.

She looked at her hands, not surprised to find them shaking. *Other people's children.* The argument was an old one, but it still had the power to hurt. Why couldn't her sister understand that Jenny considered all the children who came to her, however briefly, her own?

Impatient with herself, she pushed the hair back from her face. She wasn't likely to make Tessa understand any more than Tessa was likely to convince Jenny to give up foster care.

Not for the first time, she wondered how her parents had managed to produce two such different daughters. She knew she baffled her parents as well as her sister. She never doubted their love, but she often chafed under their expectations for her. As her mother was fond of pointing out, Jenny was twenty-eight and she *still* didn't have a husband. Her father, more subtle but no less insistent, asked when she was going to stop baby-sitting and get a real job.

They didn't understand that she loved what she was doing; caring for these children gave her life meaning. More important, it gave her love. And love was something she needed.

When she'd discovered that she was unable to conceive, she'd promised herself she would find a way to be the mother she'd always wanted to be. Unlike other girls her age, she hadn't dreamed of a glamorous career when she grew up. All she'd ever wanted to be was a mommy.

Five years ago, an article in the local paper about the need for foster parents had caught her attention. After attending a series of workshops and passing a background check, she qualified as a foster mother.

From the moment she'd taken in her first child, she knew her decision had been the right one. So far twenty-two children had stayed with her, some for as much as three years, others for only a couple of days. But Travis and Trevor had been there the longest—over four years.

She'd never regretted her decision to become a foster mom, not even when it had cost her her fiancé.

She'd met Brad Flemming just over two years ago. A loan officer at the local bank, he'd literally swept her off her feet. She hadn't been looking where she was going when she ran into him. Strong hands had caught and steadied her. Over coffee, he'd invited her to dinner.

Instant attraction, plus the fact that she hadn't had a date in more months than she cared to count, had prompted her to accept.

When she began dating Brad, she knew he didn't understand her commitment to the children. He treated her kids with a tolerance that she'd hoped would eventually grow into love. When he asked her to marry him, she believed he'd finally accepted the children and was prepared to love them as she did.

She'd accepted his ring and started making plans for the future. Only when they discussed where they'd live once they were married did she admit she'd been fooling herself.

He had tried to talk her into giving up the kids, claiming that they'd need two salaries if they were to maintain a satisfactory life-style. When she'd refused, he'd walked out on her.

She shouldn't have been surprised. Brad had always put things above people. She'd let his good looks and easy manners blind her to that.

After two days of moping, she admitted that her pride had taken a bigger beating than her heart. She'd never regretted her choice. When she'd learned that he'd taken a job with a Denver bank, she'd felt only relief. Only then had she realized how weak his chin was and the ingratiating way he smiled when he wanted his own way.

If she sometimes yearned for something more, she didn't dwell on it. Not that there was time for it anyway, she thought. A frown blunted her brows into a straight line. It wasn't a long stretch between a banker and a financial consultant. Did David and Brad share anything else beside similar careers?

She couldn't deny the attraction she felt for him. But she could ignore it. For now.

She pushed her doubts aside. The man had just arrived. The least she could do was give him a fair chance. Maybe he'd understand her love for the children and her commitment to them. For the last five years she'd filled her life with children and love. When her funds ran short, she'd advertised for a boarder and ended up with not one, but three. Now they were as much a part of the family as were the children.

She smiled, remembering the day Mrs. Abernathy showed up, with scarves floating around her and paste jewels dripping from her ears, throat, and wrists. She'd asked for a tour of the house, examined it closely, then pronounced it perfect for receiving visitations from the ''otherworld.''

Mr. Ambrose arrived shortly afterward, referred by a social worker when the retirement home where he'd lived for the last ten years closed its doors. Mr. Zwiebel, the newest member of the household, had been there only six months. But he had already established a place for himself in Jenny's heart as well as the children's.

The whole arrangement worked out perfectly except for one thing—money. There was never enough of it.

Jenny pushed her hair back from her forehead and eyed the washing machine warily. It was quiet now, almost sad-looking, as though it had received an undeserved scolding. *Like me,* she decided. Talking with Tessa always had that effect on her.

Guiltily, she looked at the phone, remembering her abrupt ending of the conversation. Tessa would expect an apology. And she would get it, Jenny promised herself. But not today. Maybe tomorrow . . . or the next day.

Two days later, David was slowly going out of his mind. A vacation had sounded good—a few weeks of rest, relaxation, leisure. What he hadn't counted on was the utter boredom that had set in before the first day was out. Of course, he could leave, go somewhere else, but he'd discovered that he didn't want to get away from Jenny and her strange household. At least not right away.

He found her hanging clothes on the clothesline in the backyard.

"Don't you have a dryer?" he asked.

"No." She shoved a bag of clothespins into his hands. "Hold this." She wrestled with a sheet covered with brightly colored dinosaurs, stretching it over the line before pinning it into place.

"Do you do this every day?"

"What? The laundry?" she asked around a clothespin she'd stuck in her mouth until she needed it. "There're seven people in our family. What do you think?"

"I meant hanging the clothes outside . . . it's obsolete."

She removed the clothespin from her mouth. "I prefer to think of it as being environmentally conscious."

"But wouldn't it be easier if you had a dryer?"

"A lot easier. But unless you happen to find a couple of hundred dollars lying around, I'll keep doing it the old-fashioned way."

"That's exactly what I'm talking about," David said triumphantly. "If you had the money, you could buy a dryer, replace the washer—"

"If wishes were fishes, we'd have a nice fry," she said, quoting her grandmother. "Unfortunately, I'm fresh out of fish."

David took the clothespin from her and turned her to face him. "I'm trying to help you."

She looked at his too-serious face, now etched with lines of frustration. "I know," she said, her voice softening. A small breeze rustled his hair, blurring the edges of the exact side part. Far from detracting from his good looks, it only drew attention to his heavy fringe of lashes and smoke-colored eyes.

Her casual attitude bothered him. He wasn't accustomed to having anyone tell him what to do, much less a slip of a woman who forgot to wear shoes.

"You sound like you're not enjoying your vacation," she said.

"It's not that. I'm just not used to sitting around. And I thought . . ."

"You thought what?"

"That maybe I could help you out. Perhaps with your finances . . . set up something quite workable. I'm really good at doing that." There, he'd said it.

She smiled, a smile that made his insides do somersaults. "That's sweet. But you're on vacation. Anyway, I couldn't pay you."

"I'm not after a salary."

"What are you after?"

"Something to do," he admitted.

"Why are you so afraid of taking some time off work?"

"Because . . ." He halted helplessly, not wanting to admit that he was afraid not to work, afraid that he'd discover he was nothing without it.

"Not a very good reason," she observed.

He agreed. It wasn't a very good reason. He looked at the woman with sunlight in her hair and magic in her smile. Was she a witch? Suddenly, he didn't care.

She was still smiling at him, her eyes wide, a dimple winking at the corner of her mouth. She was probably wondering why he was hanging around.

The answer was simple. He didn't want to leave. That realization, more than anything else, startled him into speaking.

"You're beautiful." He felt Jenny's speculative gaze on him and knew she probably thought he was mad. Or at the least still suffering from lack of oxygen. "I'm sorry. I shouldn't have said that."

"Why?"

"Because it's not the kind of thing a man says to a woman he's just met."

"Why not?"

He shook his head. "I mean . . ."

"What do you mean, David?" she asked gently.

"I don't know." That was probably the only thing he'd said since he'd met her that made any sense. "I think I'll get my things together so we'll be ready to start." At her raised brows, he added quickly, "When you are."

"You do that. I'll call you for dinner. I hope you like pot roast."

"Pot roast . . . uh, sure. Love it."

He walked away, a little less certain that he was in control of his life than he was before the encounter with Jenny.

Dinner evoked a host of memories. The large, scarred table crowded with people reminded him of his childhood. The foster homes where he lived crowded as many bodies as possible around the table.

There was a difference, though. He sought the reason. And found it when he glanced across the table.

Jenny.

The pot roast, surrounded by tiny potatoes and carrots, was familiar yet unfamiliar. How many times had he been served pot roast when he was growing up? But none had tasted like this.

Voices, sometimes querulous, sometimes demanding, pierced the air. But there were no sharp reprimands in response, only soft words and occasional laughter as Jenny turned her attention on each person in turn.

David tried to determine how she managed to make everyone feel that he or she was the most important person in the room. He had no doubt that the others shared that feeling.

Mrs. Abernathy glowed under Jenny's gentle questions about her spiritual experiments. Mr. Zwiebel beamed his appreciation as she praised him for helping Travis with an experiment, while Mr. Ambrose preened as she complimented him on his new tie.

"Jenny, tonight's the best night for the séance," Mrs. Abernathy said.

"You promised we'd have a game of checkers tonight," Mr. Ambrose reminded Jenny.

"The spirits are not receptive every night," Mrs. Abernathy pointed out. "They must come first." She directed a fierce stare at Mr. Ambrose, who folded his arms across his chest.

David looked at Jenny, curious how she would handle what appeared to be developing into a domestic crisis.

"Mr. Ambrose, I'm sure David would be a much more worthy opponent than me," Jenny said. "Why not challenge him to a game of checkers?"

The old man fixed David with a speculative look. "You up to it, youngster?"

He was trapped. Neatly trapped by a slip of a woman who gave him a wide, guileless smile.

"Sure. If the others don't need us," he hedged.

"Oh, we'll manage," Jenny assured him. "Of course, if you'd rather attend the séance . . ."

"A game of checkers sounds great," he said quickly. Too quickly, he judged, by the widening of her smile.

Two hours later, he discovered Mr. Ambrose took his checkers seriously.

"King me, king me," the old man shouted.

Grudgingly, David capped the red checker with a matching one.

"I win again," Mr. Ambrose crowed. "Ten games out of ten." He all but danced around the room before settling back in the chair to fix David with a challenging look. "You up to a hand or two of poker?"

David was about to refuse when he saw the eager-
ness in the old man's eyes. "Sure."

Mr. Ambrose pulled a well-used deck of cards from
a side table and dealt them out with surprising expertise.

David pushed his hair back from his forehead. The
evening was straight out of "The Twilight Zone." A
séance was taking place in the next room, while he
was playing cards with an eighty-year-old man whom
he strongly suspected of cheating.

Jenny walked into the room just as they'd finished
the fifth game. "All finished?"

He pushed his chair back from the table. "Yeah.
You could say we're finished."

"Beat him five games out of five," Mr. Ambrose
bragged. "Fair and square. Right?"

"Right," David agreed. "Fair and square."

"I think I'll go see what the twins are up to." The
old man shuffled off.

"You let him win," Jenny guessed when he was
out of earshot.

"No way. He won just like he said. He's got more
energy than most twenty-year-olds."

"He also cheats."

"You know he cheats?" David asked, unable to
keep the surprise out of his voice. But by now, nothing
about this woman should surprise him.

"Of course I know. We all do. But we don't let on.
It would spoil the fun. Thanks for playing with him
tonight. I know I sort of forced you into it."

"Sort of?" A smile tugged at his lips. "Don't feel
bad. I enjoyed it." He spoke the words automatically

and was surprised to find they were true. He grabbed her hand. "Take a walk with me."

"Let me go tell Mrs. Abernathy where we're going, and I'll meet you on the back porch."

David tapped his foot against the porch railing. The mountain air, which just hours ago he'd believed to be the cause of his fatigue, now filled him with a restless energy. He inhaled deeply.

"It tastes good, doesn't it?" Jenny asked, coming to stand beside him.

It did. It never occurred to him before that air had a taste. But it did. Or at least it did when he was with Jenny. Things had a way of tasting better, smelling better, feeling better, when he was with Jenny. For once, he didn't stop to analyze the feeling. He accepted it.

"You like living here, don't you?" he asked.

"It's my home," she said simply.

"Have you ever considered living anywhere else?"

"Once."

"What happened?"

"I changed my mind."

"Just like that?"

She shook her head. "No. Not just like that. I had to make a choice. I chose this." She gestured around her.

"Don't you ever get lonely?"

She laughed. "When would I have time to get lonely?"

She had a point there. With all the people in her life, there was little chance of being lonely. "What about men?"

"There's Mr. Ambrose and Mr. Zwiebel."

"And they're each pushing eighty. Do you ever go on a date?"

She shook her head. "Not very often. Pine Tree doesn't boast a surplus of single men under eighty." Her smile made him feel slightly foolish.

"I guess not."

She brushed his cheek with her palm, a fleeting caress that shouldn't befuddle his mind. Shouldn't have. But did.

"Let's go get an ice-cream cone," he said. Bright lights and noise would keep him from giving in to the need to touch her. He hoped.

"Great. I'll go tell the others."

He couldn't help the small grimace that escaped his lips.

Her face clouded. "You do want to take everyone, don't you?" An image of Brad flashed through her mind. He hadn't wanted a bunch of "runny-nosed kids" tagging along either. She'd thought David was different. Obviously, she'd been mistaken.

"Of course," David said weakly.

His feelings couldn't have been more plain if they'd been lit up in neon.

By that time, the others had heard of the proposed treat and had joined them.

"How nice of you to suggest taking us out for ice cream," Mrs. Abernathy said, patting David's cheek.

"Very decent of you," Mr. Ambrose seconded.

"Very," Mr. Zwiebel echoed.

Jenny was torn between annoyance at David and sympathy for him as her family crowded around him.

She settled for sympathy as he repressed a sigh.

Taking the whole group was a good idea, she decided, remembering the tension that shimmered between David and herself whenever they were together. With the whole family around, she didn't need to worry about things getting too personal. They'd be lucky to exchange two words without interruption.

"Let's go," Trevor urged. "We're starving."

Jenny rolled her eyes. "What about that huge piece of chocolate cake you put away at dinner?"

Trevor gave her a withering look. "That was an hour ago."

David and Jenny exchanged amused glances.

"This was the best treat we've ever had," Travis said thirty minutes later, smacking his lips.

"The bestest," Trevor said, not to be outdone.

The others added their thanks, then started toward the car until only David and Jenny remained on the bench outside the ice-cream parlor.

"Thank you for the treat," she said quietly. "They'll talk about this for weeks."

The warmth in her voice made him feel ashamed he hadn't originally planned to take the whole group. He was glad now he had. Being with the children and the oldsters, he realized how much he'd isolated himself from others. Much to his surprise, he'd had fun.

"We'll have to do it again," he said and found that he meant it.

Jenny pressed a kiss to his cheek. "Thank you."

He touched his cheek. The gentle caress moved him more than he cared to admit. And scared him. "We'd better go. They're waiting for us."

He sensed her surprise at his brusqueness. Right

now, he couldn't explain why he suddenly didn't want to be alone with her. Not even to himself.

An hour later, closeted in his bedroom, David admitted he was fighting a losing battle. He was bewitched by Jenny. Now that he knew what the problem was, he could deal with it . . . objectively and rationally. He'd approach it as he would any problem: identify, resolve, eliminate.

He settled back against the bed and pulled out a legal pad. A half hour later, he looked at his list and smiled, satisfied with his course of action. Dealing with Jenny would be no different from any other business situation.

He pulled down the sheets. The scent of lavender wrapped its spell around him, mocking all his good intentions.

Chapter Three

David paused over the keyboard of his laptop computer and watched Jenny the following morning. She was down on her hands and knees, attacking the scarred linoleum floor with a rag and scrub brush. Occasionally, she'd rock back on her heels and wipe the sweat from her face with the tail of her blouse.

"Everything all right?" she asked, looking up from her task.

"What? Uh . . . sure. Fine."

"You looked like something was troubling you."

Only you. But he couldn't tell her that. He looked at the computer and remembered what he was supposed to be doing. "I was just working out a budget for you."

Her lips compressed into a tight line.

It wasn't hard to figure out what put the frown on her face. "Hey, it's not so bad." Maybe a little humor would help. "Budget is not a dirty word."

"A lot you know," she said, returning to her cleaning.

"Why don't you tell me what you want? Then we'll design a system just for you."

"What I want is to be left alone," she said. "I don't need my family computerized."

"We're not computerizing your family," he said patiently. "Just your expenses and income."

"That won't change the fact that there's more money going out than there is coming in." All the bantering had vanished from her voice, and she pushed the hair back from her face in a tired gesture, exposing the delicate line of her neck.

"No, it won't. But it'll give you some idea of where to start."

"Okay, Mr. Expert. You win. Design away." Dismissing him with a wave of her hand, she emptied her bucket and took herself off without a backward glance.

David bit back the angry words that sprang to his lips. The lady had all but claimed he wasn't any good at his job. He'd show her just how good he really was.

Two hours later, David pushed back the pile of bills, receipts, and bank statements that cluttered the kitchen table, which he had temporarily commandeered as his desk.

"She's trying to drive me crazy," he muttered. "Strike that. She's already done it." He resisted the urge to drop the whole mess into the trash can. He'd computerized the finances of everything from small businesses to large corporations; the finances of one slightly screwy woman couldn't defeat him.

He wondered if someone had pulled an elaborate practical joke on him. Jenny's checkbook, while meticulously kept, showed a steady outgo of money with practically none coming in. What happened to the rent from her boarders, he wondered? As far as he could tell, only one rent check had been deposited within the last four months. He made a note to ask Jenny about it.

He was a financial consultant, not a magician. He couldn't make money appear where there was none.

The opportunity arrived sooner than he'd expected when she came back inside. He glanced at her, not sure what to expect after their last encounter. Her eyes were wary, but the anger he'd anticipated was absent.

"How's it going?" she asked, a bundle of what looked like weeds in one hand and a laundry basket balanced on her hip. She smelled of sun-dried sheets and fresh earth, a heady combination.

The questions he'd planned to ask died on his lips as he drank in the sight of her. Dressed in faded jeans and a peasant blouse, she looked as fresh as the Colorado morning. Golden freckles danced enticingly along the curve of her shoulders whenever she moved. Her hair fell in damp tendrils around her neck. His mouth felt unaccountably dry.

She put a hand to her hair as he continued to stare. "I must look a mess."

"No . . . you don't."

The hoarseness in his voice had nothing to do with how she looked, he assured himself. It was most likely an allergic reaction to something in the air. Funny, he'd never realized how a change in altitude could affect a person.

He cleared his throat of the lump that had taken residence there. As soon as his time was up here, he could go back to his condominium, corporate accounts, and sane life. Suddenly that life sounded bleak. He pushed away the thought. It was the life he'd always dreamed of, the life he'd spent the last sixteen years working so hard for.

He searched for something to say to take his mind off the tiny pulse that beat in the hollow of her throat. "What's that?" he asked, pointing to the weeds in her hand.

"Rosemary and lavender."

He reached out to finger the delicate leaves and purplish flowers.

"You know. Herbs."

"You grow your own?"

"I do if I want it fresh. Here," she said, and held the bundle under his nose. "Smell."

He sniffed cautiously at the familiar aroma, a scent that would forever remind him of her. "It smells like the sheets on my bed."

She smiled. "I put sachets of potpourri in the linen closet."

The scent of lavender wafted over him, and he inhaled appreciatively. It was a delicate aroma that evoked images of another century, a gentler, old-fashioned era where ladies floated about in long dresses dripping with lace.

Jenny needed someone to take care of her. The thought had him rearing up from the chair, practically knocking her over in the process. She was doing it to him again—causing him to think things he had no business thinking about. He needed to focus on helping her.

He pointed to the papers that littered the table.

"I've been going through your books. You're about

one month away from the bank foreclosing on this place.''

''I kept hoping something would happen and I could square everything with the bank.'' She smiled wryly. ''You don't happen to have a spare miracle in your pocket, do you?''

He couldn't return her smile, even though he knew she was expecting it. His anger at her attitude died before it could gather fuel. ''Sorry. I'm fresh out of miracles.''

''You don't believe in miracles?''

''Don't tell me you do?''

She nodded emphatically. ''Of course I do. If you don't believe in miracles, what do you believe in?''

''Myself. What I can accomplish with my brains . . . my hands.''

''You must be very lonely,'' she said quietly.

He started to deny it and then stopped himself. ''What if I am?''

''I'm sorry.'' The compassion in her voice angered him.

''For me?''

She didn't say anything, but he read the answer in her eyes. It made him all the angrier. He didn't need sympathy, least of all from this woman who couldn't even manage her own life. But deep down, below the anger, was something else, something he wasn't ready to face.

''Well, don't be. I get along fine without any of your so-called miracles.''

''Don't sell them short. Miracles happen all the time . . . for those who believe.''

''If you're so het up about miracles, where's one

when you need it?'' he challenged. A shadow crossed her face, and he regretted his harsh words. But maybe they'd wake her up to the truth.

''There's still a month.''

''A month.'' But his derision was wasted. Jenny was already gone, with only the lingering scent of lavender laced with sunshine to remind him that the conversation between them had taken place.

Miracles.

Only children and fools believed in miracles. She might as well have asked him to believe in Santa Claus or the Easter Bunny. Her serene insistence that something would happen shook his carefully controlled sense of order.

Doggedly, he sorted the papers, dividing them once more into neat piles of bills and receipts. Without Jenny there making suggestions and generally confusing him, the hours dragged by. Even though she provoked him, rattled him, and irritated him, he missed her quick laugh and ready smile.

A grubby hand tugged at his sleeve. ''Mr. Sherwood, Jenny says you have to come quick.''

He shoved a hand through his hair and looked up at the dirt-streaked face. Travis. No, Trevor. He couldn't tell. ''Tell her I'm busy.''

''No. You have to come. Now.'' The small, grimy hand yanked insistently at his own. Once again, the piles of papers toppled to the floor. David looked at the scattered bills and receipts and sighed. What was another hour or so?

''Where're we going?'' he asked as Travis—or was it Trevor?—pulled at him.

''Outside. Jenny says there's a miracle about to happen. She said she 'specially wants you to see it.''

Anger, quick and hot, rippled through him. Who did she think she was to try to force him into believing in miracles? It tapered off as he looked down into the earnest face, and his anger was replaced by curiosity. ''What kind of miracle?''

''Daphne's going to have a baby. Hurry.'' The small hand tugged more insistently until David had no choice but to follow.

Daphne? Not one of the boarders. Mrs. Abernathy was over eighty. Surely Jenny hadn't taken in someone else. ''Who's Daphne?''

Travis—or Trevor—threw David an impatient look. ''Our cow.''

''Daphne's a cow?'' He was going to see a cow have a baby? The feeling of having wandered into another dimension returned, as well as a twinge of impatience. He didn't have time to watch a cow have a baby. He had work to do . . . work that Jenny seemed determined he never have a chance to finish. One more look at the freckle-dusted face, though, reminded him that he was here to relax, and he gave in.

''Okay. Let's go see Jenny's miracle.''

The small hand slipped inside his. After a moment's hesitation, David closed his own hand around it.

Sharp, pungent odors of hay and animals assailed his nostrils as they entered the barn.

''David, Travis, over here.''

He followed Jenny's voice through the barn until he found her standing beside a ginger-colored cow. Random shafts of sunlight sifting through the rafters spun a golden haze over her hair, and he blinked against the effect.

"It's all right," Jenny crooned to Daphne. "Good girl. We're almost there. One more push. Hold her head," she directed David, motioning him in front of her.

"But—"

"Stroke her behind the ears. Travis, rub her neck."

David still hesitated as Travis carefully patted Daphne's neck.

Jenny threw David an amused look. "There's nothing to be afraid of."

"I'm not—"

"Shh. Just hold her and talk to her softly."

Talk to a cow? What did you say to a cow who was about to give birth? "Don't worry, Daphne. Giving birth is a perfectly natural process. Women . . . uh . . . cows have been doing it for centuries." *Uh-uh, David. You're losing it. The lady tells you to talk to a cow and you're doing it. You're definitely over the edge. Too much sunshine and mountain air.*

Daphne mooed impatiently. David imagined she was protesting the inanities he was murmuring to her. He didn't blame her.

He cleared his throat and tried again. "Uh . . . it's okay, Daphne. Everything's going to be all right." He stroked her velvety head.

"That's it, Daphne," Jenny encouraged. "C'mon, girl. You can do it. *Push.*"

Daphne bellowed soulfully before straining her pelvis one last time.

"You're doing great," Jenny praised.

"Thanks," David said, before realizing she was talking to Daphne. He felt the flush that heated his face. "I mean—"

Daphne bawled plaintively.

He risked a glance toward Jenny and saw her guide a tiny hoof out of the birth canal.

"Just a little bit more," she coaxed. "We're almost there."

A final wail of pain caused him to wince in sympathy for Daphne. "C'mon, Daphne, you can do it. Don't give up now." Embarrassed, he raised his gaze to meet Jenny's.

She spared him a quick smile before resuming delivering Daphne's baby.

"It's a heifer," she said. If she'd announced the arrival of a check for a million dollars, she couldn't have sounded happier. "Oh, David, look. Isn't she beautiful?"

"Beautiful," he said, his gaze still on Jenny. Her arms and clothes were coated with blood and mucus, but it was her eyes that held his attention. They shone with an inner light that mocked the feeble rays of the sun as it tried to pierce the shadowy dimness of the barn. "Beautiful," he repeated, his voice hoarse with emotions he refused to name.

"Help me pat her down," she said, and began gently rubbing the tiny animal with straw.

Awkwardly, David imitated her actions, gingerly patting the heifer with straw.

"Look, Daphne. You have a daughter." Jenny gently pushed the little animal forward.

Something warm wrapped itself around his heart as he watched the little heifer wobble toward her mother on spindly legs.

Tentatively, Daphne began licking her offspring, then turned to David to give him what he interpreted

as a look of gratitude. It didn't seem strange to him
that he was crediting Daphne with feelings.

The baby rooted around Daphne's teats, finally settling down to sucking noisily while Daphne mooed her
contentment. Once again, she turned her gaze to
David, inviting him, he imagined, to share her pride
in her offspring.

"What's her name?" Travis demanded.

David looked at the markings on the small animal,
identical to the ones her mother bore. "How about
Ginger?"

Travis pursed his lips in thought. "Great."

David turned to Jenny. "What do you think?" He
waited, not sure why her answer was so important to
him, only knowing that his words caught in his throat.

"I like it," she said, stroking Ginger softly.

David watched the rhythmic motion of her hand.

"Let's give them time to get acquainted," Jenny
said, and backed out of the stall.

David and Travis followed her into the light. Travis
bolted off toward the creek. Jenny perched on a fence
rail, locking her legs around a lower rung. David
propped a hand on either side of her.

"You were great back there," he said. "Do you do
this often? Play midwife to a cow?"

She shielded her eyes against the glare of the sun.
"This was only my second time. I was pretty nervous
the first time I did it."

"You handled it like a pro."

"Thanks." She smiled. "You weren't bad yourself."

He shrugged. "I just did what I was told. You and
Daphne did all the work."

She shook her head. "Daphne did the work. I was just the coach."

"You make a pretty good coach," he said, leaning closer until only scant inches separated them.

Soft color flooded her cheeks at the compliment. "Have you ever seen anything like it?" Her voice was breathless, her eyes brimming over with tears, tears he longed to wipe away.

But he didn't touch her; he couldn't, not if he wanted to maintain the distance he'd decided was crucial whenever he was around Jenny.

"Seeing a new life come into the world has to be the most beautiful thing there is," she murmured.

"Beautiful," he echoed, his gaze once more resting on her. He'd dated plenty of women, all of them talented, bright, and ambitious, each of them more beautiful than the last. But he'd never known a woman like Jenny.

She wore no exotic fragrances, and right now she smelled distinctly of barn and cow. Bits of straw still clung to her hair; her face was free of makeup and liberally streaked with dirt and God knew what else. . . . She was the most beautiful woman he'd ever seen.

She threw back her head, a breeze catching her hair and tossing it in her face.

Without thinking, he reached up to brush back the stray tendrils. He leaned closer, his lips a breath away from her skin. At the last moment, he drew back.

He raised his head and caught the bewilderment in her eyes. He didn't blame her for being puzzled. He was more than a little confused himself.

He licked suddenly dry lips. "I . . . uh . . . better get back to those bills." He planted his hands on her waist and helped her down from the fence. He let his hands linger there for a moment before reluctantly removing them.

"Of course."

The disappointment in her voice washed over him, filling him with guilt.

"I think I'll check on Daphne before I go in. I'll see you later." She headed back to the barn.

David watched her, feeling as if he'd missed out on something special. Irrationally, he was angry. The only trouble was that he wasn't at all sure whom he was angry with: Jenny . . . or himself.

Jenny attacked the barn floor with a coarse-bristled broom. Bits of straw and hay scattered; dust billowed around her. The exercise strained her already-tired muscles, but she kept at it. She needed the release of tension. Why had David run from her?

And why did it matter so much? She frowned. Everything had seemed fine. David had even relaxed the rigid control he kept on himself as they'd witnessed the miracle of birth together. Then, without warning, he'd withdrawn from her.

She propped the broom against the stall door and surveyed the results of her efforts. The barn floor looked better than it had in years, but she was no nearer to finding the answers she longed for. Comforting ones. Ones that made sense of what she was feeling. Ones that didn't leave her doubting herself.

David Sherwood was an enigma. Warm and tender one moment, aloof and distant the next. Well, he wasn't her problem. Heaven knew, she had enough of those without looking for more.

Cooperative and friendly. That would define her relationship with him from now on. No more of those almost-kisses, no more intimate conversations. And most important, no more disturbing thoughts about him to fill her days and haunt her dreams.

She wondered why the prospect depressed her so much.

Dinner was punctuated with laughter and occasional arguments. David helped himself to the plentiful food, surprised to discover he wanted seconds. Normally, he ate very little of the gourmet meals his housekeeper fixed for him. Now he was eating as if he'd been on a starvation diet.

The mountain air, he decided, was stimulating his appetite. Satisfied with the explanation, he dug into his second helping of meat loaf and mashed potatoes.

He caught Jenny watching him and flushed. "It's . . . uh . . . very good."

"I'm glad you like it."

The cool note in her voice had him frowning. The idea that he might have hurt her this afternoon troubled him. Abruptly, he pushed his plate away, his appetite gone.

Jenny didn't putter around in the kitchen after the cleaning up was done, as was her custom. He ought to be relieved, David thought, as he booted up the computer and spread out his papers. Jenny was a distraction; he could work far more effectively without her presence.

His fingers paused over the keys as he listened intently. Were those her footsteps approaching the kitchen? The smile that was still more thought than fact died when he looked up to see Mrs. Abernathy.

"Sorry to bother you," the old lady said, opening the refrigerator door. "I'll just get my glass of milk and scoot out of your way." She puttered about, talking all the while as she heated the milk and then washed the glass and pan.

His concentration shot, he admitted he wasn't accomplishing anything and headed upstairs. He paused outside Jenny's room, hoping to hear something . . . anything. Only an oppressive silence greeted him, and he made his way down the hallway to his room. As he slipped between the cool sheets, the scent of lavender attacked his senses, leaving him wanting, needy.

Conveniently ignoring the fact that he'd slept soundly for the last week, he blamed his sleeplessness on the noises of the night. A cricket serenading his mate, the gentle swish of a breeze, Daphne's occasional lowing, conspired against him.

An hour later, he gave up the pretense of sleeping. With a savage jerk, he tossed back the covers and yanked on his clothes.

He needed to find Jenny, to apologize. Maybe then he could sleep.

When he'd searched the house with no luck, he thought of the barn. He pushed open the kitchen door, startled momentarily by the brilliance of the stars. Accustomed to the suffocated starlight of the cities, he still was awed by the splendor of a mountain night.

A faint light appeared through the barn window. He eased open the door and followed the sound of a crooning voice.

Her head close to Daphne's, Jenny rubbed the cow behind the ears.

He strained to hear what she was saying.

"You're a proud mama, aren't you? You have a beautiful baby."

Daphne mooed softly.

Noisy suckling drowned out Jenny's voice.

David stepped closer, the straw lining the floor crackling under his feet.

Jenny looked up. The quick smile that lit her face faded almost immediately. He'd done that. He knew a sharp pang of regret.

"I thought you might be here," he said.

She continued stroking Daphne's neck. "How long have you been here?" she asked without looking up.

Her words made him wish he'd arrived earlier to hear the secrets only Daphne now knew. "Not long."

She nodded and turned her attention back to Daphne.

He squatted down beside her. "How's she doing?"

"Great. She's a real trouper, aren't you, girl?"

Daphne opened her eyes long enough to favor David with a benevolent look.

"She likes you," Jenny said.

The warm feeling her words generated within him surprised him. Since when did a cow's approval cause him a rush of pleasure? Something weird was going on here.

His gaze rested on Jenny's profile. The muted light of the lantern bathed her silhouette in a soft glow.

As though aware of his scrutiny, she raised her head. "Is something wrong?"

Everything was wrong, he wanted to shout. He was sitting in a barn talking with a beautiful woman about a cow's welfare. *A cow.*

Some of what he was feeling must have been reflected in his face, for she smiled up at him. "Not your usual way of spending an evening, is it?"

He laughed shortly. "Not quite."

"You need to get some jeans if you're going to hang out in barns."

His once-immaculate gray slacks were hopelessly creased and covered with bits of straw and hay. Oddly, he didn't care. Maybe because he had something far more important on his mind.

"About this afternoon—"

"Look. Ginger's trying to stand."

He accepted her not-so-subtle hint that what happened this afternoon was off-limits. Perhaps that was for the best. He didn't even know what he'd been about to say.

He watched as Daphne gently encouraged her baby, nudging Ginger with her nose. Most animals knew what to do instinctively, he reflected, but some rejected their young.

Like people.

And others gave love as easily as they breathed. Like Jenny.

He thought of the foster kids in her care. Of how she'd taken them in just as she'd taken in Mrs. Abernathy and Mr. Ambrose and Mr. Zwiebel. And him?

The thought gave him pause. He wasn't one of her strays. He was here on vacation. That was all.

Abruptly, he pushed himself up. "I'll see you tomorrow."

She gave him one of those looks that was neither disappointment nor approval. It was as if she could see into his very soul. If he even had one.

Chapter Four

He assiduously avoided Jenny the next day. With her accounts and records to go over, he'd had no trouble keeping himself busy. Now, with evening melting into night, he sought her out, not bothering—not daring—to analyze why.

A light from the porch drew him. The screen door was freckled with insects. Startled moths flitted and darted about when he opened it.

He found her there. No sunlight spun its magic over her hair now. But moonbeams, he decided, worked their own kind of sorcery. A softer, subtler kind that suited Jenny as well as the more brilliant light of the sun.

He took his time studying her. Her face was in repose now, a contrast to its usual animation. She rocked gently, swaying in rhythm to the motion of the swing.

She was singing something. He couldn't make out the words. They were foreign to him, perhaps Gaelic, but the melody intrigued him even as it soothed.

A thimble-sized yawn complemented the softness of

her voice. Katie. Moonlight touched the baby's face, haloing the silhouette of woman and child.

The sight stirred him. He remained still, loath to intrude upon the beauty he'd unwittingly stumbled upon.

''Do you want to join us?'' Jenny's voice jolted him from his thoughts.

She had known he was there all the time. The knowledge embarrassed him, but not enough to keep him away from her. He frowned, realizing the extent of the hold Jenny had on him. His plans to return to California within a month of his arrival had been discarded.

He told himself it was because she needed his help. The lie chafed against his normal self-honesty, but he didn't care. With the help of a rented fax machine and his laptop, he'd been able to keep in touch with the office and take care of anything that required his attention.

''If I'm not disturbing you.''

She patted the seat beside her. ''The night belongs to anyone who needs it.''

Her words kindled his curiosity. ''How do you need the night?''

A slight shrug shifted the baby cradled in her arms. ''The same way you need sunlight.'' She placed a hand on her heart. ''Here.''

He settled in the swing, his weight disturbing the balance so that she slid toward him. His arms steadied her. ''What do you find in the night?''

Moonbeams caught the slight tilt of her lips. ''Peace. Harmony.'' Her smile deepened. ''What do you find?''

"I don't know," he said honestly. "I never thought about it."

"If you listen carefully, you can hear the fairies singing."

If he thought she'd supply the normal small talk, he was destined for disappointment. Then he remembered. Jenny never did the expected. He started to smile, only to stop when he saw she was serious. "Fairies?"

Her hair fell across her face as she nodded. "They come out only at night. When it's safe."

"What do they do?" he asked, catching the strands of silk and tucking them behind her ear.

"Play hide-and-seek with the moon."

He wondered what he was doing sitting on a porch swing having a conversation about fairies. A week ago he'd have found something more to do with a beautiful woman. But then, a week ago, he hadn't met Jenny. "Jenny . . ."

She put a finger to her lips.

The trilling of treble notes pierced the stillness of the night.

In spite of himself, he was shaken. He didn't believe in fairies. "It's only the wind." He wished he sounded more sure of himself.

"Is it?"

Whatever he might have said was lost in the symphony that serenaded the night.

By morning, David still couldn't shake the memory of last night. The picture of Jenny and how she looked bathed in moonlight lingered in his mind with annoying persistence. Experience had taught him that the best way to exorcise a woman from his thoughts was to get to know her better.

He found her in the garden, weeding the rows of plants. A straw hat shaded her eyes against the sun, casting her face in shadow, so that he was startled by the brilliance of her smile when she looked up at him.

For the first time in years, he was nervous. "Uh . . . I wanted to ask you something."

She waited expectantly while he argued with himself.

"Will you have dinner with me tomorrow night?"

"You mean just the two of us?"

He made a show of looking around. "I don't see anyone else."

"Why?"

"Why what?"

"Why are you asking me out?"

"Because you're very pretty. And I'd like to get to know you better."

"I'd think that was the last thing you'd want."

"You're wrong, Jenny. Very wrong." He leaned over to kiss her. As kisses went, it was barely a brush of lips, yet it stirred something within him. She tasted of forgotten dreams and unspoken promises. Fresh as just-picked honeysuckle, pure as sunshine. Tenderness curled inside him.

He'd kissed women before, but he'd never before kissed one as he did Jenny. He pulled back, disturbed by his thoughts. "What about it? Will you go out with me?"

"OK. I have to warn you that Pine Tree doesn't run to much of a social life."

"I thought we might drive to Denver."

"Why so far?"

"I want to see you, be with you. Away from everyone."

A wrinkle worked its way between her brows. "Everyone?"

"You know . . . the family."

"That family is my life," she said, the frost in her voice at odds with the warmth of the day.

He felt her drawing away from him even as she said the words. "Jenny, I'm sorry. . . ."

But it was too late. She was already gone.

He'd blown it. Big-time. *Admit it, Sherwood, you're a loser when it comes to dealing with a woman like Jenny.* Maybe it was for the best. Hadn't he already decided Jenny was not his kind of woman? She was too soft, too giving, too wrapped up in the lives of others for a man like him, a man who wanted—no, who needed—all of a woman's attention to ease the loneliness inside his heart. He didn't share easily.

But it didn't stop the ache in his gut when he remembered the sweet promise of her lips. One more reason to leave the lady alone, he reminded himself. One kiss, and he was already wanting more.

Ralph hunkered down beside him. Absently, David scratched the dog behind the ears.

"You ever have woman troubles?" David asked.

Ralph yawned widely.

"Guess not, huh?"

A yelp was his only answer.

"Away from here," Jenny repeated. Her anger had vanished, but in its place was a bitter disappointment. Away from the family was more like it. If David couldn't accept her family, he wasn't the right man for her. She'd already experienced one man's refusal to accept her family. David hadn't meant anything by his dismissal of her family. It just pointed out the differences between them—the wrongness of her wanting him.

But she'd already figured that out for herself. The only problem lay in convincing her heart of the rightness of the decision.

With that firmly in mind, she felt confident to deal with her feelings for him. He was an attractive man. It was only natural that she should be drawn to him.

Sure, an inner voice mocked. And if she believed that, she was as gullible as the twins believed she was when they tried playing sick in order to skip school.

By the time she saw David again, she had things in perspective. She was responsible for her emotions. No one else. He'd made it clear how he felt. Well, she wouldn't burden him with her feelings.

She was proud of the way she managed to talk with him over dinner, as if nothing had happened. And nothing had, she realized. Nothing that mattered, anyway.

She felt his gaze on her several times. She returned it with a bland one of her own.

"Need some help with the dishes?" he asked once dinner was over.

"It's the boys' night to clean up," she said.

They reacted with predictable protests.

"Aw, Jenny. Do we have to?" Trevor whined. "We got homework."

She smiled at the standard excuse, one they'd used ever since school had started.

"We did it last night," Travis added.

"Try last week," she said. "You know the rule. Everyone takes a turn."

"Even him?" Trevor asked, pointing at David.

Jenny kept her voice pleasant but firm. "David is a guest."

Still grumbling, they began clearing the table. Only then did she realize her error. With the boys occupied and Katie playing with Mrs. Abernathy, she had no excuse to avoid David.

In the end she needn't have worried. He headed to his room with a muttered excuse that he had some work to do.

An hour later, David threw the papers onto the desk, heedless of the mess he'd just made with what had taken him days to organize. "What the heck?"

He scanned the figures once more, sure he was mistaken. A second reading confirmed he hadn't been. He rattled off a string of curses that would have earned him an ear-boxing from his third-grade teacher.

For the last six months, Jenny had not received one cent from Mr. Ambrose in rent. From what he could piece together of statements he'd obtained from her bank, the last payment from the old man had been made sometime last year.

After making sure Jenny was occupied in the garden the following morning, he decided to confront Mr. Ambrose. He found him in the kitchen playing solitaire.

David sat down beside him. "Mind if I join you?"

Mr. Ambrose grunted. "Suit yourself." David watched the gnarled hands slap down cards with enviable speed. "Mr. Ambrose, I've been going over Jenny's financial records."

The elderly man looked up briefly before returning to his game.

"Just how long do you intend to take advantage of Jenny . . . Ms. Kirtpatrick's generosity?"

A puzzled look clouding his eyes, Mr. Ambrose rubbed his jaw. "Take advantage?"

David bit back a sharp answer. "Receipts show you haven't paid rent in over six months."

"Jenny knows I'll pay her when my invention sells."

"What invention?"

"The one to recycle dryer lint. Of course, all my figures have had to be theoretical so far, seeing as Jenny doesn't have a dryer."

David stared. The old man couldn't be serious. Recycled dryer lint?

"When do you expect to have this . . . invention . . . finished?"

"In a month or so. Jenny knows. She said to take all the time I need."

David could believe that. She'd probably advanced the old man the money to get started on it.

Mr. Ambrose smiled proudly. "Jenny believes in me. She's a good girl."

David bit his tongue.

"Once my invention takes off, I'll repay Jenny everything I owe her. With interest."

This time David couldn't keep silent. "Did you know Jenny's going to lose this house unless she can come up with some money fast?"

He watched as Mr. Ambrose's normally florid face paled.

"You didn't know, did you?"

"Jenny said not to worry about the money." Mr. Ambrose pushed his glasses farther up on his nose and stood. "She always said we'd get by." He shuffled away, muttering, "I didn't know.... I didn't know...."

David sank down on the old rocker, feeling as though he'd just kicked a puppy. All the while he'd figured the old man was just out for a free ride. Now that he knew different, he didn't know what to do.

He couldn't suggest that Mr. Ambrose be evicted. And it wasn't because of Jenny. He just couldn't do it. This house and its crazy inhabitants were getting to him. A wry smile pulled at David's lips. Jenny would probably call it one of the miracles she was so fond of. All he knew was that he cared about the old man. Maybe because Mr. Ambrose reminded him of the grandpa he'd always longed to have.

David shook his head in disgust at what he was going to do.

Once more the feeling of falling through the looking glass returned as he made his way down the hall. He knocked at Mr. Ambrose's door and waited. He listened as the jazzy beat of "Boogie Woogie Bugle Boy" drifted through the door.

Mr. Ambrose opened the door. "I'll be gone as soon as I finish packing."

"Look, Mr. Ambrose, I'm sorry for what I thought. ... I didn't realize.... I'll loan you the money until your ... invention sells."

Mr. Ambrose drew himself up. "I don't take charity. Never have. Never will. Not even during the Depression. Martha and I made do. Ate beans and salt back for nigh on a year. You young folks don't know what hard times are." His eyes misted in remembrance before hardening as they once more rested on David. "If you say Jenny's in trouble because of me, I'll clear out. Only honorable thing to do."

David saw the open suitcase on the bed, a small stack of clothing next to it. He settled on edge of the bed, pushing the clothes to one side. A carefully mended rip in a shirt caught his attention. The shirt said more than words ever could about the older man's financial straits. And his pride.

He couldn't let Mr. Ambrose leave. Not only would Jenny never forgive him; David strongly he suspected he'd never be able to forgive himself.

"It's not charity. It's a loan."

"I don't take loans," he said with quiet dignity. "Jenny and I had an arrangement."

David resisted the urge to wipe his brow. He couldn't let the older man see how important this was to him. That would make him too vulnerable. "You got anything against making a business deal?"

Mr. Ambrose gave David a suspicious look. "Depends."

"That's all a loan is. A business deal. I'll even draw up a contract, if you like."

A slow smile spread across Mr. Ambrose's wrinkled face, only to fade and be replaced by a frown. "Can't let you do that. It could be years before my invention sells. Even longer than that before it starts making real money."

"Think of all the interest I'll collect," David said, keeping his voice properly grave.

The old man rubbed his chin. "Well, if you put it that way, maybe we could work something out after all." He held out his hand with quiet dignity.

With equal dignity, David shook the wrinkled hand.

"This is right nice of you, son. Right nice." Then the old man directed a fierce scowl at David. "Just don't try any funny business. I know all about you big-city fellows with your fancy contracts. I don't aim to be hornswoggled. I'm not some country hick, you know. You'll have to excuse me now. Bladder's not what it used to be."

"Now, just a minute," David said, but Mr. Ambrose was already shuffling toward the bathroom.

After a hurried trip to the local bank, David reappeared with the money. He waited while Mr. Ambrose painstakingly signed his name on the contract David had hastily drawn up, and then he pressed the money into the weather-beaten hands.

"This is just between us," David reminded Mr. Ambrose. "We don't want Jenny to know."

"Why not?"

David searched for a plausible answer, wondering whether he was trying to convince the old man or himself. "Because she might worry. We don't want that."

Mr. Ambrose pressed his finger to the side of his nose. "You're right. Jenny would worry. She's a nice girl. Always thinking of others." He regarded David with sharp eyes. "You're a right nice feller. Too bad you live in the city. Never could abide cities. No heart to 'em. They ain't got no heart a'tall."

No heart.

Mr. Ambrose's words echoed through David's mind for the remainder of the day. Was that what was wrong with his life? No heart?

He thought of his condominium, decorated by one of the city's top design firms. Predominantly chrome and glass with stark white carpet and walls, it had about as much personality as his office—zilch.

Unbidden, the image of his room at Jenny's house, with its hand-hooked rug and four-poster bed, appeared in his mind. No one could accuse it of lacking personality. It was the same in all the rooms of the house. They reflected Jenny—her warmth, her generosity, her essence.

Angrily, he pushed away the thoughts as if he were somehow being disloyal to what he'd worked for. Wasn't that what he wanted? A successful career, a richly appointed house, all the trappings of success? A month ago, even a week ago, he'd have said yes without hesitation. Now, he wasn't so sure.

"You're losing it, man," he said, his voice harsh against the silence. "You're losing it big-time."

It couldn't be put off any longer.

Discovering how Jenny supported Mr. Ambrose was easy. It had taken a little more digging to unearth how she was subsidizing her other two boarders. He still couldn't believe it.

Instead of bringing in money by renting out rooms, Jenny was actually losing money. Then again, knowing Jenny as he did, he ought to have guessed why so much money was going out and so little coming in.

Now he had to confront her with what he'd found out.

He caught her just as she was on her way to the barn. "We need to talk."

"Can't it wait?"

"No."

Her brows rose at his uncompromising tone, but she settled on the porch swing.

He held up a bill. "What's this?"

She glanced at it. "Dentures."

Her casual tone didn't fool him. "I can see it's for dentures. What I want to know is who it's for. You don't wear dentures." He paused. "Do you?"

"Of course I don't wear dentures. They're for Mrs. Abernathy."

"But why did you pay for them?"

All at once, she appeared uncomfortable. "She gave me some cash, and I wrote a check for them."

"Liar."

She glared at him. "It's the truth."

"Look at me and then say that."

She tried—he'd give her that—but she couldn't get the words out.

"Jenny, you're the poorest liar I've ever known."

Her chin jutted out defiantly. "All right. I paid for them. When she lost her other set of dentures, she wouldn't even come out of her room, she was so embarrassed. She couldn't eat anything but baby food. I couldn't let her starve, could I?"

She didn't say any more, but he could hear her thoughts as clearly as if she'd spoken them aloud. *So there. What are you going to do about it?*

He wanted to take her in his arms and kiss her; he also wanted to shake some sense into her.

He settled for pointing to the next item. "A twenty-seven-inch color TV. The one in the living room is a nineteen-inch black-and-white. Do you mind telling me why you need two TVs?"

The second television resided in Mr. Zwiebel's room. David wanted to hear her reasoning behind this one. As always, Jenny managed to surprise him.

"Did you know Mr. Zwiebel used to play in the pros? Watching baseball on TV is the only thing that gives him pleasure these days. He can't watch it with the children running around. So I bought a TV for his bedroom."

"And of course you had to get cable for him?"

"A lot of the games aren't broadcast on regular channels."

It all sounded perfectly reasonable. She'd dug herself neatly into debt helping the very people who were supposed to be a source of income for her. How could he possibly help dig her out again?

"What about their families? Mrs. Abernathy showed me pictures of her grandchildren, so I assume she has children. And Mr. Zwiebel has at least one daughter that I know of."

Jenny smiled sadly. "Did you look closely at those pictures she showed you?"

"No. . . ."

"They're over fifteen years old. Her family hasn't been in touch with her for at least that long."

"How do you know?"

"I talked with the social worker who worked at the retirement home where Mrs. Abernathy lived before she came here. In all the time she lived there, she never had a visitor, not even a letter. The only mail she ever gets here is her social security check.''

David wanted to swear. When he was a child, he'd have given anything for a family, someone to love and be loved by. And others threw it away with scarcely a thought. He wanted to hit something. Preferably someone. He settled for slamming his fist into his open palm.

''How can families stop loving each other?'' she asked.

His own pain was forgotten as he heard the anguish in Jenny's voice. He gathered her to him, wishing he could protect her from what he'd learned early in life: Love was an illusion.

He'd spent the first half of his life wishing for parents to love and to love him back. He'd spent the second learning that the love he craved didn't exist.

He covered her hand with his own, not knowing what else to do. His experience in offering comfort was limited, at best. ''They get too busy with their own lives, their own problems,'' he said at last.

''Have you noticed how Mr. Ambrose checks the mail every day?''

David nodded. He'd seen the old man shuffling out to the porch, waiting impatiently for the mail to arrive.

''Do you know what he does afterward? He goes back to his bedroom and rocks in his chair. I knocked on his door one time and found him that way. I tried talking with him, but he wouldn't answer. He just kept rocking. Then, a couple of hours later, he was back down in the basement, working on his inventions, like nothing happened.''

David blinked rapidly. Must be something in the air.

His eyes felt watery, sensitive. The tears that fell were foreign to him. He wiped his cheek and looked at the drops that clung to his fingers in wonder.

She brought his finger to her lips and sucked away the tear. The gesture would have been very sensual if he hadn't been hurting inside. "It's all right to have feelings, David," she said, her voice soothing his raw emotions with the balm of her compassion.

"Yeah. Says who?" But his joke fell flat, and he winced. He sounded as if he were begging for sympathy. He hadn't begged for anything since he was six years old and asked his father not to drink. Begging had only earned him a backhand across the face. He'd resolved then and there that he'd never ask for anything again.

"Me."

He managed a smile. He should have known it wouldn't fool Jenny, though.

"Is it because of what I said?" she asked.

"No. Not you. Never you." He captured her hand in his own, bringing it to his mouth. He wanted to kiss it, but then remembered he had no right. He settled for skimming his lips across her knuckles. "What are we going to do about Mr. Ambrose and the rest?"

"Do?"

"You can't keep supporting them."

"I thought you understood—"

David held up a hand. "I'm not suggesting you throw them out. I'm trying to come up with a way they can support themselves."

"Mr. Ambrose's invention—"

"To recycle dryer lint?" This time David's smile was genuine. "You don't believe in that, do you?"

"Maybe. It could work, couldn't it?"

"Not in a million years. I'm afraid we're going to have to do better than that."

They spent the next hour trying out ideas, some of them serious, others hilarious. David forgot his resolve to straighten out her finances as he tried to outdo Jenny in outrageousness.

"You're crazy," he said at her last suggestion that they invent a machine to track down missing socks and make a million dollars selling it.

"It's the company I keep."

"Jenny . . ."

Apparently she sensed what he couldn't put into words, for she leaned over to brush her lips against his.

The moment she touched him, the second her mouth settled on his, he stiffened. Seconds stretched into minutes, and still he didn't dare respond. He felt her confusion and knew he was lost.

He returned the kiss, no longer caring about whether or not he had the right, his hand cupping the back of her neck, bringing her still closer. When he raised his head, he kept his arms around her.

He kissed her once more. "This is reality."

"Don't you believe in anything?"

"Myself. What I can see and touch."

"What about love?"

David pulled back. "What about it?"

"It's the ultimate reality."

He looked into her eyes and knew he was playing with fire. Women like Jenny wanted promises for happily-ever-after and all that went with it. He wasn't made for that. He didn't even believe in love, so how was he supposed to promise it?

"I'm not what you need." He'd spoken nothing but the truth. Why, then, did he wish he could take back the words?

"How do you know what I need?"

"You need someone who'll be around for the long haul. You need someone who wants the same things you do—a home and family. That's not me."

"How do you know?"

"Do you know where I grew up?" He didn't wait for her answer as the old pain washed over him. "In a foster home. Funny, isn't it? Only it wasn't a home. It was a prison. A prison without bars."

"I don't understand—"

"You wouldn't. You'd never understand the kind of people who take a kid in for money."

The soft gasp that escaped her lips made him regret his outburst. At the same time, it made him angry. He didn't want pity. Least of all from her. His anger faded as abruptly as it had flared to life. Jenny had too much pride of her own to feel pity for someone else.

"I'm sorry," she said. The compassion in her voice was echoed in her eyes.

He was tempted, sorely tempted, to accept the understanding he saw in her eyes, but pride kept him from responding to it.

"For what?"

She cupped his cheek, her soft palm fitting itself to the rough stubble. "Making you remember."

"What makes you think I'm remembering anything?"

"Your eyes. They tell me you're hurting."

He had no answer to that. No answer that he could tell her, anyway. And so he remained quiet.

"Don't," he said when he could bear the silence no longer.

"Don't what?"

"Don't feel sorry for me. It was a long time ago. In a way, I'm grateful to those people. They taught me not to count on anyone but myself."

"It doesn't have to be that way," Jenny said, drawing him back to the present. "You were hurt. Badly. By people who didn't care. But not everyone's like that." Her fingers curled around his arm.

He looked at her, disturbed by the compassion he saw in her eyes. His gaze lowered to the small hand resting on his arm, the fingers unadorned by jewelry, the nails unpolished. It wasn't that he'd never felt a woman's hand on his arm before, but this was different.

It shouldn't have moved him, but it did, this small gesture of comfort. *She* moved him. He shook off her hand and pretended not to notice the hurt in her eyes.

She'd only been trying to help, and he'd thrown it back in her face. He ignored the tug of remorse he felt at his callousness. That was who he was, what he was. If she didn't like it, then that was too bad. The sooner he was out of here, the better.

She turned and walked away.

"Jenny, wait—"

But she'd already gone.

David waited for the relief he was sure to feel. He'd done the best thing . . . the only thing. So why did he feel like the world's biggest jerk? And why did he feel like he'd come out the loser?

He attacked the question with the same analytical skills he used to attack all life's problems.

He cared about Jenny. Well, all right. He could live with that. Caring was a natural human emotion. That he'd experienced so little of it in his life didn't mean it didn't exist.

Caring was acceptable. A man could care about a woman without losing himself in her.

Not a woman like Jenny, an inner voice whispered.

He silenced it. Caring was acceptable, he repeated. And caring was all he felt. It was all he *could* feel. Jenny Kirtpatrick was off-limits. She came with wedding bells, a household of people who depended upon her, and a truckload of responsibilities.

The wanting to be with her all the time, the needing to hold her, the tugging at his senses whenever she was around, wasn't love.

Dragging a hand through his hair, he sighed, remembering the hurt look on Jenny's face. They had to talk. And after they did, everything would be back to normal. The only problem was, he wasn't quite sure what normal was anymore. A number of days at Jenny's house had him doubting her sanity. Or his.

All the more reason to complete the help he had offered and go home. He wondered why he found the idea so depressing.

The following morning, he found Jenny alone in the kitchen, cleaning up after breakfast. If she remembered the circumstances of last night, she appeared to have put it out of her mind. To his chagrin, the gaze she leveled at him was serene.

"Cereal's on the table," she said, returning to her task.

"We need to talk."

"Funny. I thought we did that last night."

His jaw tightened. She wasn't going to make this easy. "I was a jerk."

She looked up briefly from where she was wiping off the counters. "You're right."

"That's all you're going to say?"

"What else is there?"

"I'm sorry."

The admission was out before he knew that he planned to say it. It must have surprised her as much as it did him, for she gasped softly, dropping the dishrag she'd been using.

A small smile inched across her lips. "Was that so hard?"

He thought about it. "Not as hard as I thought it would be."

"Congratulations."

"For what?"

"You're making progress, Sherwood."

He stared at her. It couldn't be that easy. He hadn't been exaggerating when he said he'd acted like a jerk yesterday. She ought to be yelling at him or crying or something.

But she only smiled at him and asked, "How about some breakfast?"

He was about to protest that he wasn't hungry, when he realized that he was. "Only if you sit down and let me fix it. You've waited on enough people already," he said, eyeing the sinkful of dirty dishes.

She hesitated for just a second, then plopped down

in a chair. "That's the best offer I've had all morning."

He was no whiz in the kitchen, but he could make
a fair omelette. Whistling softly, he set about the task,
conscious all the while of Jenny watching him.

"You're pretty good at that," she said as he beat
the eggs with a wire whisk.

"For a bachelor, you mean?"

"For anyone."

The simple words of praise sent warm color rushing
into his cheeks. He knew enough about Jenny to know
she never said anything she didn't mean.

He popped bread in the toaster, poured juice, and
set the table. While he watched her eat, he wondered
how many times anyone had waited on Jenny. Not
many, he guessed. She worked too hard. But he had
no right to tell her that.

For the span of the meal, he forgot about everything
he had been doing lately. He forgot that Jenny came
with more ties than a beribboned Christmas present.
For a few stolen moments, they were just a man and
a woman enjoying each other's company.

And he savored each moment of it.

Her lips puckered slightly as she drank the juice,
drawing his attention to their fullness. Lately, it
seemed everything about her intrigued him, down to
and including the most innocent gesture. *Get a grip,
man,* he told himself silently, even as he dreamed of
kissing those same lips. They'd be lush, still tasting
of juice, and more intoxicating than the most exquisite
champagne.

At that moment, she looked up, and he couldn't
mistake the shimmer of attraction before she did

her best to bank it, to give him that maternal, composed look once more. He wanted to take up the challenge she unknowingly issued. Her lips, still moist from the juice, beckoned him to taste of their sweetness.

The return to reality came swiftly as Mrs. Abernathy wandered into the kitchen, looking for her crystal ball.

"It'll show up," she said, apparently unconcerned when she didn't find it. She looked from Jenny to David. "It's hot in here." The knowing expression in her eyes caused him to push his chair slightly away from Jenny's. The older woman floated out on a sea of scarves, perfume, and suggestion.

Jenny stood and began clearing the table. She dumped the dirty dishes into the sink and began washing.

He picked up a dishtowel. With a quick nod of thanks, she handed him the clean dishes.

"Thanks," she said. And he knew she was thanking him for more than the breakfast.

"You're welcome."

The prosaic words mocked what they'd shared earlier. Try as he would, though, he could think of nothing else to say.

"I'm going to work in the garden," she said, drying her hands. "What about you?"

"I need to go over some papers. I'll see you later?" He made a question out of the last and ignored his need to follow her outside.

"Sure." The intimacy that had existed between them only minutes ago was lost. She jammed a straw hat on her head and forced herself to walk away. She couldn't fight him right now, couldn't continue to try to pry his heart open.

David had more sides than a multifaceted diamond, she decided. Warm and giving one moment, cold and remote the next. He deliberately kept her at arm's length, as if he were scared of letting her too close.

The idea that David might be afraid caused her to stop what she was doing. The more she thought about it, the more convinced she became that she was right.

It didn't excuse his hot- and cold-running feelings, but it went a long way to explain them. And as much as he tried to pretend otherwise, she knew he wasn't indifferent to her.

Maybe if she found a way to sneak past all those defenses he'd erected, she might find the real David Sherwood. The glimpses she'd managed to catch of him were enough to convince her the result would be worth the effort.

Chapter Five

"And they lived happily ever after." Jenny closed the book and smiled at the children.

"How do we know they lived happily ever after?" Travis asked.

"Because it says so," Trevor answered. "All books end that way."

"Not all," Jenny said. "Just some of them. The happy ones."

Katie snuggled further into Jenny's lap. "You liked it, didn't you?" she asked, tickling Katie's stomach.

Katie rewarded her with a gurgle followed by a hiccup.

Jenny patted Katie's diapered bottom. "C'mon, sweetie. It's bedtime for you and your brothers."

"Aw, Jenny," Travis and Trevor moaned together.

"I'll take Katie for you," Mrs. Abernathy offered.

Jenny settled Katie into the waiting arms. "Thanks. I don't know what I'd do without you."

The old lady beamed. "Come on, Katie. Do you

want to wear your duck sleeper tonight or the bunny one?''

Katie babbled.

''Duck,'' Travis interpreted.

''Rabbit,'' Trevor said.

''I'll be in in a minute to tuck her in,'' Jenny said to Mrs. Abernathy. She turned to the twins. ''C'mon, you two. School tomorrow.''

''Don't remind us,'' Trevor said on an exaggerated moan.

''Yeah,'' Travis seconded. ''Don't remind us. School. Yuck.''

Jenny struggled to suppress a laugh at the fierce scowls stretched across their faces. ''Yuck or not, you still have to go.'' She kissed two freckle-dusted cheeks. ''Get ready for bed and I'll come in to kiss you good-night.''

They trudged off, muttering something about frog-faced teachers.

She chuckled. School had been in session for three days. Every day had brought about a new set of complaints from the boys.

''Can't you find something better to read to them?''

She whirled around to find David watching her, a scowl twisting his lips. ''Something better?''

''Something *real*.'' He gestured to the book of fairy tales.

''This is real,'' she said, tapping the book.

''It's a fairy tale. How can it be real?''

''The feelings in it are real. The fact that people care about each other, love each other, grieve for each other is real. What can be more real than that?''

"Fairy tales make everything come out right in the end. Real life's nothing like that. You're setting those kids up for disappointment."

"If I'm setting them up for anything, it's to expect good things. That's half of being happy."

"What's the other half?"

A soft smile traced her lips. "The other half is being happy."

His frown intensified. "What's going to happen when they find out that real life's not like that?" He didn't give her a chance to answer. "They'll figure they've been cheated. They'll blame you. And they'll be right."

"What do you suggest I read to them? *Time? Newsweek? The Wall Street Journal?*"

"Anything that shows them what the world is really like. If they don't learn the facts now, they'll be handicapped for the rest of their lives."

You're the one who's handicapped. But she couldn't tell him that. He'd reject it just as he'd rejected every overture she'd made to get him to open up.

"What is the world like, David?" she asked instead.

Shadows appeared in his eyes, hinting of pain and loneliness. She wanted to touch him, to comfort him somehow, but she knew better than to offer anything that smacked of sympathy. David had erected so many barriers that she sometimes despaired of breaching them. But she would, she promised herself. One at a time, she'd bring them down.

She remained silent, hoping this time would be different, hoping . . . She held her breath.

He flicked on the television. "This," he said, gesturing to the screen. "This is the world you should be preparing them for." A major network broadcast the news of the day. More fighting in the Middle East. A murder. A celebrity couple announced their divorce.

She winced as one grim story followed another until she could stand it no longer and turned off the set.

"What good is filling their heads with a bunch of fairy tales going to do them?" He grabbed her arms and pulled her closer.

"What good is filling their heads with violence and pain going to do?"

An angry hiss escaped his lips as he released her. "You don't understand, do you?"

"It's you who doesn't understand."

"I understand all too well." He dug in his pocket and held up a fistful of bills. "This is what they need to learn. How to make a living, how to take care of themselves. So they'll never have to beg for anything."

Her heart bled at what he'd unwittingly revealed. "Did you? Have to beg?"

His eyes, filled with anger only moments ago, frosted over. She preferred the anger. It, at least, was alive.

"Don't practice your do-gooding on me, Jenny. I don't need it."

Regret washed over her. This wasn't the day that she'd find the key to healing the scars of David's past. Still, she had to try. She gestured to the money he held in his hand. "It's not everything."

"No. It's not everything," he agreed. "But it's the most important thing—having enough money so you don't go hungry, having enough money so the landlord can't kick you out of a one-room apartment that should have been condemned years before, having enough money so the bill collectors don't harass you.''

His words in the last few minutes told her more about his past than he had in the last couple of weeks. Huge blanks still remained, though. She decided to risk a question. ''What was your family like—before the foster homes?''

The shutters came down so fast that she stepped back. She'd trespassed. The message was as clear as if he'd spoken the words aloud.

''I don't have one.''

Whatever she expected, it wasn't this. The pain she'd prepared herself to hear was missing. There was no emotion at all. The very absence of it made her ache for him all the more.

''My mom died when I was six. After that it was just the old man and me. Until he took off. That's my father—short on responsibility and long on feeling sorry for himself.''

She strained to catch the next words.

''Like me.''

''David.'' She stretched out her hand. ''Let me help you. Please.''

''I don't need your help.''

''You need it more than you know. Did you ever wonder why you ended up here?''

''I'm friends with your sister and brother-in-law. They recommended your place for a nice vacation, away from everything.''

''Tessa and Jack know *lots* of people. Why did *you*, in particular, end up here? Why not someone else? Maybe you were *meant* to come here.''

"I'll bite. For what?"

She hesitated. He wasn't going to like this. "Because you need help."

"Yours?"

She remained silent.

"Lady, I'm not the one whose house is about to be sold out from under her. My life's in order."

"Your life is so sterile you're afraid to let a feeling inside. You're so afraid to admit you might have feelings that you'd do anything to hide them."

"You're way off the mark."

His anger fueled her determination to convince him otherwise. "Am I? Everything that happens, happens for a purpose. Why is it so hard to believe that you were sent here for a special reason?"

"You know why I came here. You're talking in riddles."

"Maybe."

"Better watch it or you'll start sounding like Mrs. Abernathy."

"Despite everything, Mrs. Abernathy still believes in life . . . in love. Do you?"

"Don't start practicing your miracles on me. I'm immune to them."

"Just like you're immune to love. Right?"

"I'm not immune to it. I just don't believe it exists."

She reached up to cup his cheek. "I'm sorry, David." She'd gone too far. She knew it as soon as the words were out of her mouth.

His eyes grew remote and cold, his gaze chilling her as he removed her hand as if he couldn't bear her touch. "You're great with little kids and old people,

Jenny, but you're way off base with me. Better stick to what you know.'' Without a backward glance, he walked away.

She could only stare after him and wonder if she'd ever find a way to his heart. The sigh that trembled from her lips was more of a sob. She clamped her hand to her mouth and wiped her eyes.

The children would be waiting for her. She wasn't up to explaining away tears to them.

In the end it wasn't the children who commented on the telltale redness around her eyes, but Mrs. Abernathy. The old lady assessed Jenny with a sharp glance and put down her crystal ball. ''It's him, isn't it?''

Jenny wanted to deny it but settled for the truth. ''Something's hurt him. I wish I could help him.''

''You can,'' her friend said, patting Jenny's hand. ''Just be there for him when he's ready.''

Ready for what? Jenny wanted to ask. But Mrs. Abernathy had already returned to her crystal ball, calling up the spirit of her dead husband.

Jenny tumbled into bed that night, more confused than ever. Mrs. Abernathy meant well, but she didn't understand just how unapproachable David could be when he put up barriers around him. He would always resist making himself vulnerable and admitting that he might need anyone.

Though he'd told her precious little about his childhood, she'd guessed that he'd had to learn early to depend on only himself. The woman brave enough to love him would either have to accept the defenses he'd built around his heart—or break her own heart trying to breach them.

Love, the kind of love between a man and a woman that bound them together forever, wasn't likely to be part of the future for herself and David.

Which meant she'd be smart to ignore the attraction she felt for David Sherwood. She was honest enough to admit that she needed much more from a man than the kind of casual affection David seemed determined to offer. Nothing less than true commitment on every level would satisfy her.

Unless a miracle occurred, she feared David would never be able to give more than a guarded portion of his heart. If that.

David rubbed his palm against his cheek, trying to wipe away the warmth left by Jenny's touch. Instead, the action only served to remind him of the softness of her hand. From there his thoughts took him to the compassion in her eyes. Compassion for him.

He swore softly. He didn't need her sympathy or her help. His life was following the plan he'd set out for himself. In a few more years, he'd have enough money to retire.

And then what?

The question startled him. He'd never before considered what he'd do after he reached his goal. Now the possibilities intrigued him. More, they frightened him. Why hadn't he ever given any thought to the future beyond that?

Because he didn't have one.

The answer came with alarming swiftness. Automatically, he discounted it. He was upset after his encounter with Jenny. He wasn't thinking clearly. He wasn't . . .

All his rationalizations fell flat.

Why couldn't she leave him alone? She wasn't like other women he'd known. She simply asked questions.

And more often than not, he found himself answering them.

At the first question, he'd given her a look that said clearly, ''Back off.''

But she'd only smiled and waited. Maybe it was her smile. Maybe it was the way she didn't push. He wasn't sure what it was about her, but he ended up telling her things. About himself. About his life. About his *feelings*.

Before he'd known what was happening, he'd told her more about his past than he'd ever shared with anyone.

His childhood was a stark reminder of what happened when he let his feelings out. Giving in to his emotions inevitably led to disappointment. To pain. And, finally, to disillusionment.

Bits and pieces of the past merged together to form a collage of memories. His first foster family. Wanting to believe he'd found a home, he'd reached out to the couple's son. The boy, only a year older, had taunted David, claiming his parents had only taken David in for the money they received each month.

The second foster home was different. The family there seemed genuinely to want him. His tentative efforts to open up were met with gentle encouragement. Just when he started to feel accepted, he was transferred to another home. After that, he kept to himself. He'd learned his lesson. Too well. If he didn't find love, well, that was the price he paid for protecting himself.

The absence of love was a small price to pay to ward off pain. He'd had enough of that.

His thoughts spun back to Jenny. The last thing he needed was some woman trying to restructure his life. Even if she did have eyes like melted chocolate and lips that begged to be kissed.

He had to get away from her as quickly as possible. If he had any sense at all, he'd just head back home. He waited for a sense of relief to come with this very logical plan.

It didn't.

In fact, the idea of leaving held remarkably little appeal. All the more reason to wrap up his efforts on Jenny's budget and get out of here. With that in mind, he pulled out his laptop computer and started making notes for tomorrow, ignoring the chime of the clock. His earlier tiredness slipped away under his new urgency to finish. The sooner he had a handle on a way to help Jenny get her finances in order, the sooner he was out of here.

The anticipation left him feeling cold inside.

The following morning, he arranged the piles of bills on the table with a precision at odds with the rest of the comfortably cluttered kitchen. Trevor's science project claimed most of the counter, while Jenny's dried herbs hung from the ceiling. Katie's high chair occupied the corner, competing with a small table holding Mrs. Abernathy's crystal ball. A smile creased his face as he recalled how she'd moved the ball from the living room to the kitchen, claiming the ambience was better there.

When Jenny walked in, carrying Katie, he rose automatically. "I thought we could—"

"Oh, good, you're here," she said.

The warmth that suffused him at her words vanished abruptly as she handed Katie to him.

"Can you feed Katie? I've got to help Trevor finish his project before he goes to school."

David found his arms filled with baby and his papers shoved to one side as Jenny placed a bowl, spoon, and bib in front of him. "Thanks."

He stared down at the baby in his arms in utter astonishment and not a small degree of fear. "Uh, Jenny . . ."

Katie began to whimper. Outraged shrieks greeted his attempt to smile at her. Not that he blamed her. It was a ghastly attempt, at best. Fear dissolved into sheer terror.

"Pat her back," Jenny said, pulling the high chair into place by the table.

He did as instructed. The baby's howls mellowed to damp, shuddering sighs. When she produced a small, beatific smile at him, he felt he'd passed a major test.

Jenny rewarded him with one of her own smiles, the kind that turned his insides to jelly, and said, "Just put her in the high chair. She'll take it from there."

Juggling Katie in one arm, he yanked at the tray. When it clattered to the floor, he gave what he hoped was a confident smile and put the baby into the seat. Holding her still, he slid the tray in place.

He watched with growing horror as Jenny poured a gray mixture into the bowl. He eyed the mess from a healthy distance. "You really expect her to eat this stuff?"

Jenny's smile widened. "Don't worry. She likes it."

He wished he shared her confidence. His fingers felt clumsy as he tied the bib around Katie's neck, working it beneath her double chin. Cautiously, he lifted the spoon to Katie's mouth.

She spit the cereal back at him.

A direct hit.

He wiped his eyes. "Okay, Katie. Let's try it again." For every three spoonfuls, he figured he managed to get one inside of her. The other two ended up on Katie's face, sleeper, the high-chair tray, and him.

"Wow! David's feeding Katie. You gonna do this every morning?" Trevor asked.

Busy shoveling cereal into Katie's mouth, David only glared at the boy.

"Come on, Trevor," Jenny said. "Let's get this finished. And then you've got chores to do before you go to school. It's your turn to sweep the floor."

Predictably, he groaned. "But I wanna watch. This is more fun than any old science project."

She gave him a steady look before he nodded. "Okay, okay," he muttered.

David dodged another volley of cereal, earning a giggle from Katie.

Occasional grumbling from Trevor punctuated with encouragement from Jenny filled the next half hour. David marveled at her patience and breathed a sigh of relief when they pronounced the project finished.

"I'm outta here," Trevor called once he'd finished

his chores. He balanced the volcano in his arms and headed out the door.

"Congratulations are in order," Jenny said, plopping down in a chair beside him. "I managed to survive a science project and didn't lose my cool." She sounded as happy as if she'd just won the lottery.

"Congratulations," he said as he slid the last bite into Katie's mouth.

The baby gurgled happily, slapping the tray and sending bits of spilled cereal flying.

David looked at the latest blob on his shirt without even a flinch. It matched the others already decorating him. He could feel Jenny's gaze on him. He looked up and saw the amusement in her eyes.

"Now it's my turn to say congratulations." Her voice sobered. "And thank you. I'd never have managed without you."

Her words gave him a rush of pleasure.

"It looks like Katie shared some of her cereal with you," Jenny said, dabbing at his shirt with a dishrag.

"Maybe I'd better wash up."

Her smile did funny things to his insides. "Maybe you should. I'll clean Katie up."

At the sound of her name, the little girl lifted her arms and began babbling.

David watched as Jenny nestled Katie to her, uncaring of the goop that transferred itself from the baby to her. "You . . . uh . . . you're getting cereal on your clothes."

She looked unconcerned. "They'll wash."

"Yeah, I guess they will."

He thought about Jenny's indifference toward clothes while he showered and changed. How many other women could help a nine-year-old finish a volcano, cuddle a cereal-smeared baby, and still look as fresh as a summer morning? None that he knew.

"You look like you again," Jenny said when he reappeared in the kitchen.

He gestured to the pile of bills on the table. "About these bills . . ."

She waved them away. "Maybe later. We haven't got time right now. We're going to pick apples."

"Jenny, this is important. We have to . . . What did you say?"

"We're going to pick apples."

Pick apples? A mental picture of sharing the task with her was unexpectedly appealing. "But the bills—" he felt compelled to protest.

"Can wait. Today's an apple-picking and picnicking day."

"What's an apple-picking day?"

She dragged him over to the kitchen door and threw it open. "Look. Feel."

He looked. And felt.

The day sparkled. Sun shimmered off the tin roof of the barn. A breeze, no more than a puff of air, really, found its way through the open door. The heavy scent of flowers past their prime perfumed the air.

She was right. The day was begging for a picnic.

She pulled a wicker basket from a cabinet and began filling it with an assortment of food. "I thought we'd take the ham left over from last night." She looked up. "How does that sound?"

"Great." But his mind wasn't on food. It was on the fall of hair that brushed Jenny's cheek. It was on the softness of her voice as she hummed an off-key tune.

"What about Katie?" he asked, wondering if this outing were to be a twosome or a threesome. At the moment, he wasn't sure which he preferred.

"Mrs. Abernathy volunteered to watch her."

Jenny scraped her hair back from her face and twisted a rubber band around it. With her hair in a ponytail, she looked about twelve years old.

She hefted the picnic basket. When he made to take it from her, she stopped him. "I have something else for you to carry. In the barn."

He followed her to the barn, where she spent a few moments nuzzling Daphne and Ginger and Sheila before pointing to a splintered ladder. He eyed it dubiously. "You're not going to use this thing, are you?"

"Sure. Don't worry. We're not going far, and it's not very heavy."

"That's not what I'm worrying about." But his words were lost as she whirled away and gathered up three bushel baskets. She stacked them together, fitting the picnic basket inside the top one.

"Come on," she called.

"What's the rush?" He tucked the ladder under his arm and hurried after her.

She spread her arms, the gesture encompassing the earth and sky. "This day is too good to waste a minute."

She was right. The first hint of fall hugged the air and gilded the trees.

Tucked in the hillside to the west of the house, the apple orchard hummed with the constant buzzing of bees.

"Don't worry," Jenny said. "They won't bother us if we don't bother them." She pointed to a gnarled tree laden with fruit. "We'll start with this one."

He leaned the ladder against the tree, more alarmed than ever. The tree loomed over them. The ladder creaked ominously as he tested it. "You're kidding, right? You're not going up there."

She gave him a surprised look. "Why not?"

"It's not safe."

Her laugh rippled around him. "You're sweet when you're being overprotective."

Sweet? The last thing he was feeling was sweet. "I'll go."

"Don't be silly, David. You'd never make it. The ladder won't hold you."

She was right. The rickety ladder looked scarcely able to hold her weight, much less his.

"I'll be perfectly safe."

"Jenny, wait. . . ."

His words went unheeded as she scrambled up the ladder as agilely as one of the children.

"Don't worry," she called down to him. "I've done this dozens of times."

Don't worry, he fumed. She was twenty feet above the ground on top of a ladder that looked at least as old as Mrs. Abernathy.

"It's great up here," she called down. "You can see for miles."

"Get the apples and get back down here," he yelled back.

"Spoilsport."

He watched as she stretched out on a branch to better reach the fruit. She filled the cloth bag tied around her waist quickly. "Coming down," she hollered.

The ladder shifted against the tree as she started to back down, and he gripped the sides of it. "Haul your cute little self down here right now or I'm coming up after you." It was an empty threat, and they both knew it.

Her sack bulging with fruit, she turned and gave a jaunty wave. His heart jumped to his throat when she swayed slightly. He was two rungs up before he realized she was nearly down. He settled his hands on her hips, helping her down the rest of the way and holding her against his chest. His breath shuddered to a sigh as he assured himself she was safe.

He continued to hold her. "You ever do something like that again and . . ."

She kissed him.

He forgot what he'd been about to say in the sweetness of her lips as they brushed against his. Automatically, his hands came up to grasp her arms.

She felt small and vulnerable in his arms, her kiss fresh and genuine . . . just like the woman herself. Gently, he released her.

She gave him an odd look before turning a smile on him. "Let's go find another tree."

He picked the next tree, ignoring Jenny's protest that it was too small. All he cared about was that it was low to the ground. Soon they had the three bushel baskets overflowing with apples.

"Time for lunch," she announced.

In the shade of a tree, they spread an old patchwork quilt on the ground. They feasted on cold ham, potato salad, and chips, washing it down with homemade lemonade.

"Now for dessert." She rubbed an apple against her sleeve and handed it to him.

His tongue curled as the tart juice slid over it. "It's good," he said between bites.

"There's nothing better than a just-picked apple." An apple crunched between her teeth.

"You do this often?"

"Only in the fall," she said, her eyes bright with laughter. The amusement in her eyes spilled over into her voice.

"You're laughing at me." He was surprised to find himself wanting to laugh with her.

"Only a little," she admitted, her voice full of fun. "Fall's when apples are harvested."

"You caught me. I'm a city boy."

"But a quick learner."

In no hurry to get back, they spent another hour in the cool shade. The day was filled with the kind of magic he'd come to associate with Jenny.

To his surprise, David found himself sharing his childhood dream of painting, a dream he'd nearly forgotten. Funny he should think of it now. He looked up to find warm encouragement in Jenny's eyes. Maybe it wasn't so funny after all.

"Why don't you?" she asked.

"Why don't I what?"

"Start painting again. Maybe even sell some."

He laughed, ignoring the flash of interest deep inside. "In case you haven't noticed, most painters don't exactly make a living. Unless they paint houses."

"So?"

"So, starving's not on my list of preferred activities," he said lightly.

"Who says you're going to starve?"

"The statistics—"

She made a rude sound.

"That doesn't make them wrong."

"It doesn't make them right, either. Dreams do come true—if you want them enough."

It was just one more example of the fairy-tale kind of thinking Jenny was so fond of. But he couldn't help wondering what would have happened if he'd had the courage to try making his dream come true.

"What kind of painting did you want to do?"

"Portraits," he said without hesitation. "When I was a kid, I liked to mess around drawing people's faces."

"Did you keep any of your sketches?"

"They're packed away somewhere, I guess," he said, needing to end this conversation.

To his relief, she let the subject drop. He wondered what his life would have been like if he'd had someone like Jenny by his side, quietly urging him on. Maybe he'd have taken the chance and tried making a living with his art.

He almost snorted at the idea. He could just see himself as a starving artist living in a ratty attic apartment. No, he'd made the right decision when he'd decided to go into business. It was a practical choice, a sensible choice. That he was good at what he did made the choice all the more logical. And he didn't dislike what he did. So why was he defending it, even to himself?

The sun slipped low in the sky. Jenny began packing up the basket. He didn't want the day to end. Not yet.

Leaves crackled as he laid her back against the ground. Dappled light touched her skin, highlighting the smattering of freckles across her nose. He longed to kiss each of them. Tenderly, almost reverently, he brushed her cheek with the pad of his thumb.

Her hair captured the colors of the leaves; amber and russet vied for dominance. "You're beautiful," he said, a hitch in his voice.

"I don't need compliments."

"And I don't give them. I was simply stating the truth."

She angled her head and traced her lips over his.

It took three trips to haul the bushels of apples, ladder, and picnic basket back to the house, but David didn't mind. It meant more time spent with Jenny.

Now where had that come from? Hadn't he decided only last night that he needed to finish up and get out of here before he did something stupid? Right now he wasn't prepared to define *stupid*. But then he justified his thoughts by telling himself he was storing memories for when he did leave—memories that would get him through when the dark hours of loneliness crept up on him.

Still, he wasn't disappointed that his plans for going over the bills had been postponed. Spending the day with Jenny was as close to heaven as he was likely to get.

After dinner, he was ready to call it a day. His muscles were weeping with fatigue. He'd just tell Jenny good-night and . . . He sniffed once. Twice. His mouth began to water. The kitchen, redolent with spices and cooking apples, beckoned.

"Watch your step," she called. "The floor's sticky."

David slipped his way across the floor to the table. "Don't sit—"

He sat, then frowned at the wet stickiness that seeped through his neatly pressed slacks.

"I'm sorry," she said. "I'm making applesauce. Some of it got on the chairs and I haven't had a chance to wipe them off."

He grimaced as he pulled away from the chair. "It's okay. I've still got three pairs of pants left."

She chuckled, a soft ripple of sound that made him think of mountain streams and summer rain showers.

"You make your own applesauce?"

Stirring a bubbling mixture on the stove, she nodded. "It's a lot better than the stuff you buy in the store." She dipped a spoon into the pot and held it out to him. "Careful. It's hot."

He took a cautious bite. It was like no applesauce he'd ever tasted before. Rich with cinnamon and nutmeg, it was thick and chunky. "It's good."

"Just good?" Her need for his approval was hovering in her eyes.

"It's great."

"Want some more?"

He wanted, but not what she was offering with her spoon. That had him stepping back. "Uh ... no, thanks. I'm pretty wiped out."

The warmth of her smile almost made him change his mind. He wanted to stay so badly that he knew he needed to step away.

He took the stairs two at a time, as if demons were

snapping at his heels. Once inside his room, he sighed heavily. That had been close. Too close.

Not bothering to remove his pants, he sank onto his bed, groaning slightly as his muscles protested their unaccustomed workout. It was a good kind of tired, he decided. The kind that came from honest labor.

Though he was exhausted, sleep eluded him.

Pictures of Jenny filled his mind. Her eyes laughing down at him as she perched on the ladder. The softness of her mouth as she bit into an apple.

Why had he told Jenny about his dream of painting? He'd never shared that part of himself with anyone before. He'd kept his sketches in a small carved chest that his mother had given him before she died. A lock had insured privacy.

A couple of times he'd thought of showing some of his better drawings to a teacher, but something always held him back. Pride. Fear of ridicule.

Once again, he wondered how his life might have been different if he'd had someone like Jenny in his corner. His sigh was filled with annoyance. Worrying over what might have been wasn't his style. Tomorrow was his thirty-fifth birthday. One of those milestone birthdays that caused him to pause and reflect on his life. Ordinarily he didn't pay much attention to birthdays. They came and went with regularity. This one, though, felt different. Maybe *he* was different.

He dismissed the idea as soon as it materialized. To acknowledge it would be to give credence to the possibility that Jenny was right about him wanting something different out of life.

Angrily, he punched his pillow. Jenny Kirtpatrick was the last person he ought to consult about changing the course of his life. The woman couldn't even balance her checkbook. She was disorganized, unrealistic, and too generous for her own good. She was also beautiful, warm, and giving.

He swore softly. It was time to get the heck out of Dodge.

Chapter Six

"Happy birthday!"

"Happy birthday!"

The shouts and cheers reached his ears before he was even inside the front room. Were they for him? He looked about, taking in the homemade decorations. A birthday party? His brow wrinkled as he tried to remember the last birthday party he'd had. His sixth . . . right before his mother died.

He looked at Jenny.

"We all planned it," she said, kissing him lightly on the cheek.

"How did you know?"

"My sister told me."

"Pretty sneaky."

"Yeah." She looked smugly pleased with herself.

Travis pulled at Jenny's sleeve. "Hey, you two gonna talk all day or we gonna have a party?"

"Let's party!" Trevor said.

The twins handed David a package.

"Open it," Travis ordered when David hesitated. "It's for you."

"Me?"

"Yeah," Trevor said. "We picked it out ourselves."

David looked from one earnest face to the other and felt a rush of affection for them. "Thank you."

"You can't thank us yet," Travis said with nine-year-old logic. "You don't know what it is. What if you don't like it?"

"I'm sure . . ." David continued staring at the package. When was the last time anyone had given him a gift? Long enough ago that he couldn't remember.

"You need some help?" Trevor asked eagerly.

"Trevor," Jenny began in a warning voice.

"It's all right," David said. "I'm sort of out of practice at this sort of thing." The quick tears in Jenny's eyes had him regretting his choice of words. "Hey, it's all right," he said for her ears alone. The last thing he wanted was to put a damper on the party.

"You gonna open it or not?" Travis's impatient words dragged him back to the present.

"Let's do it," David said.

Within seconds, the boys had ripped off the wrapping paper.

"A football."

"Do you like it?" Trevor asked, a hint of uncertainty making his voice higher pitched than usual.

" 'Course he likes it, dummy," Travis said. "Who wouldn't like a great gift like that?"

"I love it," David said, meaning it.

Mrs. Abernathy pushed a large box toward him.

"Open mine next," she said, sounding as eager as the boys.

With the twins' help, David opened the next present and lifted out a fisherman's sweater. Reverently he fingered the hand-knitted garment. "You made this? For me?"

"Of course it's for you."

"It's b—" He cleared his throat. "It's beautiful." He leaned across the table to plant a kiss on her rouged cheek. "Thank you."

Mrs. Abernathy beamed. "You're welcome."

With the accompaniment of the boys' shouts and Katie's giggling, he opened a latest best-seller from Mr. Ambrose and an autographed copy of a 1952 game program from Mr. Zwiebel.

"Hey, there's one more," Travis called, handing David a large, bulky present. "It's from Jenny."

"This goes with it." She handed him a card.

He slipped it from its envelope and read the message inside. "Dreams can come true." Giving her a quizzical look, he tore the paper aside. When he lifted out a sketchbook, a set of charcoals and pastels, and oil paints, he could only stare.

Now he could do what he'd been thinking about all night. He could capture Jenny's likeness on paper. Or at least he could try. Then, when he left, he'd have a small piece of her to take with him.

He raised his gaze to meet hers. "Thank you." The words mocked him with their inadequacy, but Jenny didn't appear to notice anything wrong with them.

"You're welcome."

"Paper and crayons," Trevor said in disgust. "What kind of gift is that for a guy?"

"Come on, you two," Mrs. Abernathy said, shooing them into the kitchen. "You can help me set out the cake and ice cream." With a wink at David, she herded the two older men along with the boys.

David raised his brow. "Cake and ice cream?"

Jenny slipped her arm in his. "Can't have a birthday party without 'em."

He turned her in his arms. "I don't know what to say."

"You don't have to say anything." She reached up to kiss him. "All you have to do is blow out the candles."

"Candles, huh?" The anticipation in his voice had him smiling sheepishly. "Could you fit them all on?"

"Thirty-five's not so many."

His gaze strayed to the art supplies. "You really want me to try this?"

"I want you to be happy."

The simplicity of her words was at odds with what he saw in her eyes. There he saw a myriad of emotions—compassion and need and more love than he dared to believe existed.

"Hey, Jenny, David," Travis called from the kitchen. "You guys coming or what?"

"We'd better go," Jenny said.

"Yeah." Reluctantly, he let her go. Now wasn't the time to try to decipher what he read in her eyes. He wasn't sure if the time would ever be right.

Alone in his room after the party was over, he removed the party hat Mrs. Abernathy had insisted he wear, smiling as he remembered how she'd placed it on his head herself. He liked the old lady and the two elderly gentlemen. He even liked the twins and Katie, which was funny, since he'd always felt awkward around little kids and avoided them whenever possible. They'd all welcomed him into their tight-knit group with a warmth that shamed his standoffish attitude. Today was just one more example of their acceptance.

A birthday party was the last thing he'd expected. For that reason alone he should have known. A smile twitched at his lips. Jenny always did the unexpected. It was one of the things he liked best about her.

The thought caused his brow to furrow. He was getting in too deep. If he didn't know better, he'd think he was falling in love with her. But he was safe. As long as he remembered he didn't believe in love, he was all right.

"I'm sorry I'm so late getting this to you, Jenny. I didn't know—" Abruptly, Mr. Ambrose cut short whatever he'd been about to say. He thrust some bills into her hand.

She scarcely gave them a glance, expecting a token payment on his rent. When the amount registered, she barely contained her surprise. In her hand was six months' rent.

"But how did you—"

"It's all there," he said. "You can count it. If I'd known . . ."

"I don't need to count it. If you'd known what?" she prompted gently.

"Nothing." He shuffled from foot to foot.

"You're sure you can afford this right now? If not, I can—"

"I can afford it just fine. You've been carrying me

too long as it is.'' He kept his gaze fixed on the floor, clearly reluctant to meet her eyes.

Her curiosity aroused, she was about to press the issue, when she realized he was uncomfortable.

''You're a real sweet girl, Jenny, worrying yourself about an old man like me. You ought to be spending your time sparking. Maybe with that young feller in there.'' He jerked his finger toward the kitchen, where David was reviewing accounts. ''He ain't bad, for a city feller.''

''You're not old,'' she declared, ignoring the heavy-handed hint about David.

''Thank you for that.'' He kissed her cheek, and she caught a whiff of Old Spice and lemon drops. As he walked away, she noticed he held his shoulders a little straighter than before.

Where had he gotten the money? As far as she knew, he had no other income other than his regular social security checks. And why his persistence in paying her today? She hadn't shared her money worries with anyone except David.

David.

The pieces fell into place. David must have told Mr. Ambrose about her plight. A slow anger kindled inside her as she thought of him bothering the old man for back rent. If he'd badgered sweet Mr. Ambrose about money . . . she shook her head as the theory fell short. It still didn't explain the money. Unless . . .

Her anger ebbed as she realized what must have happened, and a warm feeling settled around her heart.

David Sherwood, you're a fraud, she thought. *A gold-plated fraud. And you've just been found out.* How had she ever thought he might be like Brad?

She hugged her newfound knowledge to her. She'd keep his secret. For now, anyway.

Jenny had been acting strange lately.

Not that she hadn't been acting strange before; after all, her whole household was strange. This was a different kind of strange.

Good analysis, Sherwood. The lady's got you so tied in knots that you can't even think about her without getting muddled.

If he didn't know better, he'd say she knew of his little loan to Mr. Ambrose. He'd sworn the old man to secrecy and didn't believe he would break his promise to keep the transaction just between the two of them.

Still, Jenny had been smiling more than usual, the kind of smile that said *I know something and you don't know I know.*

Obviously, she and the rest of her offbeat family were affecting his reasoning powers. What he needed was a day away from here. A trip into the city should do it. They'd have lunch there, make a day of it. It'd do Jenny good to get away for a short time.

He pulled up short as he realized how he'd automatically included Jenny in his plans. Wasn't the whole idea to get away from her and her crazy family?

Immediately, that part of him that needed to explain everything kicked in. He was a man; Jenny was an attractive woman. It was only normal that he'd want to spend time with her. Away from the distractions of her family and responsibilities.

But how to convince her to take the day off? A smile worked its way across his lips. Jenny could never resist a plea for help. All he had to do was tell her he needed her help in picking something out for the boys. He'd learned that their birthday was coming up in another month.

Just as he'd known she would, Jenny readily agreed to help him. Her delight in something as simple as a shopping trip was infectious, and he soon found himself caught up in the quest for just the right present for the twins.

A display of sports equipment captured his attention. He wandered over to it and fingered a leather mitt.

"I noticed the boys have to share a mitt when they play ball," he said to Jenny. "I thought maybe I'd get them each one of their own."

She glanced at the price tag and gave a small gasp. "They cost the earth."

He shrugged, the cost meaning very little to him. "Leather mitts will last a long time. Think of them as an investment."

He saw her wavering.

"Please . . . I *want* to do it."

She reached up to press a kiss to his cheek. "You're nice."

"Nobody's ever called me nice before."

"That's because they don't know the real you like I do."

Uncomfortable with the turn of the conversation, he picked out the mitts, added two bats, and handed the saleslady a credit card. When the transaction was completed, he turned back to Jenny. "Now what would you like?"

"I don't need anything."

"I didn't ask what you needed. I asked what you'd like."

"There is one thing," she said.

"Name it."

They took the escalator to the lower floor of the mall. "Those." She pointed to the display case of a bakery. "Chocolate chip–macadamia nut cookies."

"You're kidding." Every other woman he'd ever dated would have asked for something much more expensive.

"Uh-uh. I'm crazy about them."

He bought a dozen and tried to sort through his feelings. Jenny was so simple, so pure—so happy.

She pulled two cookies from the bag, handed him one, and bit into the other. "Heaven," she said with an appreciative sigh.

He brought her hand to his lips, ignoring his own cookie. Her lips widened as he licked the gooey chocolate from her fingers. Nothing could match her taste. Instead of releasing her hand, he laced her fingers in his. Her hand felt small, fragile inside his. His pulse scrambled. Could she feel it? Did she know what she did to him?

They explored the various shops along the street, their linked hands swinging between them. For the first time in his memory, he felt peace.

"Hungry?" he asked after they'd covered the length of the open-air mall.

"Starved."

He'd noticed an exclusive-looking restaurant a few blocks back. "I saw just the place." He wanted to spoil her.

Jenny frowned when he tried to lead her inside.

"Something wrong?"

"No . . ."

"Out with it."

"It looks a little stuffy," she whispered. "Besides, it's probably awfully expensive."

He started to tell her that he wanted to take her someplace special, but she'd already whirled away. Reluctantly, he followed.

"This looks perfect," she said, pointing to a place he'd overlooked.

Flanked by a boutique on one side and a bookstore on the other, it wasn't a restaurant at all but a small diner, with its hand-printed menu listed in the window.

The diner was a far cry from the upscale places usually favored by his dates, but the food was excellent and the service prompt. Once again he reminded himself not to compare Jenny to other women. Inevitably they came out the losers.

Uninterrupted by the demands of children and boarders, the meal was quiet. They shared and laughed, lingering over coffee until David signaled for the bill.

Outside, Jenny grabbed his hand. "C'mon. There's something I have to see."

His groan was more reflexive than annoyed. The boutique. What woman could resist the lure of beautiful clothes? But for Jenny, he'd suffer through even that. His indulgence changed to surprise as Jenny dragged him into a tiny shop tucked between the boutique and a men's store.

The shop looked like something from another century. Ribbons and lace curled over hardwood counters. Dried flowers hung from the ceiling, while live blossoms spilled from buckets and bins, their heady scent a welcome relief from the heat of the day. A china doll held a nosegay in her hands. Old-fashioned postcards and prints decorated the walls.

"Smell," Jenny said, holding a basket in front of his nose. "Rose petals. Don't they smell heavenly?" She moved from one bin to the next, reminding him of a butterfly flitting from flower to flower.

Watching Jenny's delight in the various pots and jars sparked a glimmer of an idea. He struggled to control his growing excitement while he sorted through the pros and cons.

A familiar aroma teased his nostrils, distracting him. "What's that?" He frowned, trying to identify the fragrance.

"Lavender. You know, the stuff I dry from the garden."

That was it. Lavender. A scent he would forever associate with Jenny.

"How much does it cost to grow this stuff?" he asked, sifting his fingers through a pot of lavender-scented potpourri, knowing he would fill his sterile condo with it when he got home.

"Hardly anything. I grow my plants from seed." She fingered a length of pink satin ribbon, drawing it across her cheek, her pleasure in the simple act obvious.

He doubted she had any idea how appealing she looked, and dragged his thoughts back to the idea that was nagging at his mind. Women, in twos and threes, browsed and sampled creams and oils. Most of them, he noticed, ended up buying something.

"Have you ever thought of marketing your pot-pourri and sachets?"

"You mean selling them?" She shook her head, turning her attention to a bolt of lace. "I give them to my friends."

He kissed the tip of her nose. "Of course you do. But you need a way to make money. Look around you." He watched as she took in the notion.

Her brow puckered. "Do you think I could?"

"I don't know why not."

"You're crazy. Do you know that?"

"Maybe. But I know a great opportunity when I see one." He grabbed her and swung her around.

"David, would you please slow down?" she said breathlessly when he set her down. "We don't even know if there's a market for what I make."

He gestured around him. "This is your market. This and other stores like it. They've got to buy their things somewhere. Why not from you?"

"Why not?" Enthusiasm sparked her eyes, her skin was flushed, and her lips . . . her lips begged to be kissed. He yanked his thoughts back to what she was saying.

"There's lots of things I could make. Fragrant oils. Herb vinegars. Fancy pillows. I can do it. I know I can. There's so much I want to do for the kids. . . . Trevor and Travis are going to need braces soon. And they're growing so fast that they're out of their clothes practically before the tags are off. We could get the house painted and a new roof and—" She broke off. "Have I spent the first million yet?"

"Not quite." He grinned. She was beginning to catch the vision. Now if he could only convince the bank to give her an extension on her mortgage. His smile dissolved as he thought of the money required to get the business going.

"What's wrong?"

"Nothing that can't be worked out."

"It's money, isn't it?" she said flatly.

"We'll think of something." He saw the light slowly die in her eyes and mentally kicked himself. Why hadn't he thought through the scheme before raising her hopes like that?

"We'd better be going," she said in a subdued tone.

"We'll find a way," he promised. "We'll make it work."

She gave him a faint smile.

When they reached the house, he pulled into the driveway, turned off the engine, and looked over at Jenny. Light and shadow played across her face. Her lips were parted gently.

He kissed her.

"Thank you for a wonderful day," she said, her voice no more than a thread of sound. She let herself out of the car, not giving him a chance to respond.

Even after she'd soaked in an herb-scented bath, sleep refused to come. Ideas to market her products spun through her mind. David had planted a seed of hope, one that refused to die in the face of all her doubts.

Her excitement built even as reason cautioned her to slow down. It took money to start a business. And money was something she didn't have, never would have. If only David hadn't planted the idea. If only he hadn't come into her safe little world and disrupted everything. But then, she wouldn't trade the joy of knowing David for all the peace in the world.

She pulled on a robe and tiptoed down to the kitchen. Might as well do something productive.

Twenty minutes later, her hands covered with flour, she jabbed the bread dough with a vengeance. Punch, fold, punch again. Slowly, painfully, her thoughts began to quiet. The dough stretched under the kneading until it finally turned smooth and satiny. With a few quick twists, she shaped it into loaves and set them on a towel to rise.

"You always bake bread in the middle of the night?" a deep voice asked.

Startled, she whirled to find David watching her. "Only when I can't sleep."

"Why?"

"It helps pass the time."

He gave an impatient shake of his head. "Why can't you sleep?"

She started washing the dishes. "Too many things on my mind."

"Like money?"

"Like no money."

He rolled up his sleeves and moved closer.

She resisted the urge to step away. "You don't need to help."

"I want to."

Apparently sensing her confusion, he touched her cheek. "It's all right, sweetheart. We'll make it all right." He plunged his hands into the soapy water and started washing.

She picked up a towel and began to dry the dishes

he handed her. Caught up in her thoughts, she didn't realize they'd finished until his voice registered.

"Jenny? We're through."

"Oh." She fumbled for something to say but drew a blank.

He took the towel from her and hung it on the refrigerator door handle. "I have the perfect cure for insomnia."

To her surprise, he led her out to the porch. He settled onto the swing and patted the seat beside him. "C'mon." He draped one arm across her shoulders, pulling her closer. "We'll find a way to make it happen."

Nestled against him, she was tempted to believe him.

Her head cautioned her to run as far as she could as fast as she could, but her heart betrayed her, ending her earlier ambivalence. If this was to be all she had with David, then she'd grasp it with both hands and be grateful for it.

Chapter Seven

David hadn't meant to listen to Jenny's side of the telephone conversation, but something in her tone snagged and held his attention.

"Yes, I understand. . . . I'll have her ready. About nine o'clock."

He saw the spasm of pain cross her face as she recradled the receiver. He started toward her, knowing whatever it was, it was bad. And nothing could stop him from comforting her.

"Tell me," he said softly, blocking her retreat with his body.

She stared at him for a long moment, tears pooling in her eyes. When one spilled over, he felt his heart shatter. "Katie's being adopted."

Her pain filled him.

"I can't let them. Not yet. She's still a baby. I can't lose her. I can't." Panic rose in her voice, and she tried to push past him.

He halted her by placing his palms against her cheeks. "You knew it had to come."

Her hands came up to grasp his wrists. "I know. But I didn't think it would be so soon. I love her." Her voice broke on that, and she swallowed a sob.

"I know, sweetheart. I know." He closed his arms around her, letting her tears soak his shirt.

"You don't understand." She held up a hand when he would have protested. "I can't have children. Trevor and Travis and Katie, all of them—they're my children."

Reeling from the news she'd just given him, David folded his arms around her. A woman like Jenny, unable to bear children? It must have torn her apart. Now he understood her commitment to her foster kids.

"Don't feel sorry for me," she said quietly. "I came to terms with it a long time ago."

"And that's when you decided to become a foster mother?"

Her nod was jerky. "I need to tell the others. Will you come with me?"

"Do you have to ask?" Anger at what he couldn't change, regret at what he wanted to change and didn't dare, welled up inside him. Using his thumbs, he wiped away her tears. "You care too much."

She pushed away and looked at him with eyes awash with pain. "I don't know how to be any different."

No, she'd never be able to stop herself from caring, from loving, even out of a sense of self-preservation. "When will they pick her up?"

"Tomorrow."

Not much time. He suspected there wasn't enough time in eternity for Jenny to say good-bye. "Will you get to meet the adoptive parents?"

"I don't know. Maybe. Why?"

"If you saw Katie was going to a good home, maybe you could let go of her."

Jenny's shoulders slumped. "I know she'll be going to a good home, to people who want her, who'll love her. It's not that."

"What is it?"

"I love her." Her voice stumbled over the words, and he tightened his arms around her.

"I know, honey. I know." He rocked her back and forth, trying to absorb her pain and knowing he couldn't. Silently he cursed his helplessness. She needed him, and he couldn't do a thing to help her. Except hold her, be there for her.

She felt small and delicate in his arms. The eyes she lifted to his were soft and vulnerable and tear-shiny. He drew in a sharp breath.

Let go of her, a voice ordered. *Step back before you do something you'll regret.*

It was too late. He was already doing it. And it was too late for regrets.

His lips touched hers. She was quiet in his arms. Slowly, he lifted his head. Cupping her shoulders, he set her back only enough so that he could see her face.

What he saw there caused the breath to knot in his chest. Love. So much love that he could lose himself in it.

His choice of words startled him. Lose himself. If he gave in to whatever it was he felt for Jenny, he would most certainly lose himself. In her. In the love she gave so effortlessly. In her life.

The picture his mind painted was enough to have him easing her away from him still farther. He couldn't afford to be caught in the web of love surrounding Jenny. It would reach out and seize him in its grasp. He had a feeling he might never find his way free. He knew Jenny would never intentionally set out to ensnare anyone. So why was he so afraid? If he had any smarts at all, he'd get out of here before he got in any deeper than he already was.

But how could he leave her when her heart was being ripped apart? The answer was simple: He couldn't.

Aware that she was looking at him oddly, he drew her to him once more. As his arms closed around her, he knew he had lost—one way or another.

"Let's go find the others," she said.

Dry eyed, Jenny told the rest of the family about Katie. "We knew she couldn't stay here forever. She's going to a home where people will love her."

"But we already love her," Travis said.

"I know, sweetheart," Jenny said, slipping an arm around his shoulders. "I know."

Trevor and Travis didn't hide their tears; nor did the oldsters. Mrs. Abernathy openly wept while Mr. Ambrose tried to comfort her. Mr. Zwiebel rocked back and forth.

Trevor fisted his hands at his sides. Travis gave a hiccuping sob before throwing himself into Jenny's arms. The elderly boarders gathered around Jenny. David prepared to step back, to let her family grieve with her, until he realized they had enfolded him into their circle. A crack appeared in the wall he'd built around his heart, a crack he was no longer certain he wanted to close up.

Tears ran freely. The twins'. Mrs. Abernathy's. He

touched his cheeks, surprised to find them wet. Everyone cried but Jenny.

Apparently sensing something was wrong, Katie became fussy. Jenny nestled the baby to her, crooning nonsense words until Katie settled down.

"Let me take her," Mrs. Abernathy said, reaching for the little girl. Singing an off-key lullaby, Mrs. Abernathy left the room.

Eventually, the others followed until only Jenny and David remained.

"It's all right," he murmured, reaching for her again. "You don't have to be strong anymore."

Great, heaving sobs tore at her body as she let him support her both emotionally and physically.

When her breathing slowed and the occasional sob subsided into sighs, he lifted her and carried her to bed. He removed her shoes, tucked the covers over her, and prepared to wait out the night with her. She didn't sleep. He knew because he'd lain beside her, counting her every breath—wanting, needing.

Morning came all too soon.

The turmoil of getting the boys off to school distracted her for a short time. The oldsters each said their good-byes to Katie, then disappeared to grieve in their own way. Then all there was left to do was wait. Thank heavens David was there to share the silence with her.

The social worker arrived promptly, bringing with her a young, obviously nervous couple.

"Jenny, this is Mary and Tom Ellison," the worker said.

After introductions and pleasantries were exchanged, Jenny brought Katie from her room.

"She's adorable," Mary said, reaching out for Katie. "Just as I imagined."

Jenny pressed a final kiss to the baby's forehead and tried not to feel. That the heart was being ripped out of her made the task next to impossible, but somewhere she found a smile and forced it to her lips. Her arms felt hopelessly empty without Katie.

"Thank you for loving her," the young wife said, cuddling the child close. "I know how hard this must be for you."

She doesn't know the half of it, Jenny thought. Couldn't they see how this was tearing her apart? Couldn't they . . .

"Is there anything else we should know about her?" Tom asked, tickling Katie's cheek.

"She gets a little fussy at night," Jenny said, setting out Katie's few belongings. "But if you rock her to sleep with her blanket, she'll settle down in a few minutes."

"I'm sure Mary and Tom will know how to comfort her," the social worker said, gently urging them to the door.

Jenny's eyes glistened with tears, but she managed to keep her smile. She couldn't resist one last kiss and reached over to kiss Katie good-bye. "Please . . . love her."

"We will," Mary promised, the happiness in her eyes almost destroying Jenny.

The door closed.

David was there for Jenny when she came apart. He didn't hesitate, just slipped an arm beneath her knees and around her shoulders and carried her to the porch swing.

"I know they'll love Katie. Why can't I be happy for her?"

"You are."

"How do you know?"

"Because I know you. Maybe better than you know yourself."

It was true, she thought a short while later as her hand went limp in his. She *was* happy for Katie. And for the young couple who would become her parents. Her breathing slowed, dried tears leaving trails down her cheeks.

She stretched and shifted in his arms, snuggling further into his embrace. She liked the feel of his arms around her, strong, comforting, protective. Ordinarily, she didn't let people protect her; she was too busy protecting them. But, sweet heaven, it felt good, if for but one self-indulgent moment.

When Jenny awoke, she was in her bed, a quilt covering her. She rubbed her eyes, blinked a couple of times, and looked at the clock. Four o'clock.

She'd slept most of the day away. Not surprising. She dragged herself into the shower. The stinging spray revived her body, if not her spirit.

The mood downstairs didn't need added gloom. Her family needed her, perhaps more than ever. And she didn't intend to let them down.

"I declare this a holiday," she said upon entering the kitchen.

The boarders and twins turned to her, their expressions disbelieving.

"But Kate . . ." Travis began.

"Katie's happy," Jenny said gently. "She has another family to love her now. That doesn't mean we stop loving her, only that we get to share her." Jenny blinked away the moisture that glazed her eyes and gave her brightest smile.

"Jenny's right," Mrs. Abernathy backed her up. "Katie will always have a place in our hearts, but we have to let her go."

"I vote we go out for ice cream," Trevor said. "Katie loves ice cream," he added, his voice wobbling a bit.

"Good idea." Jenny cupped a hand on his shoulder and squeezed lightly. "Let me tell David."

She found him in the barn. The murmur of voices led her to Ginger's stall.

"You're living up to your name," she heard him say. "You're the color of the gingersnaps my mom used to make."

The little animal mooed softly. And Jenny knew that David had finally taken a big step toward finding happiness.

The tender scene locked in her mind, Jenny cleared her throat. "We're going out for ice cream. Do you want to come with us?"

"Ice cream?"

"Ice cream is Katie's favorite," she said simply.

David's admiration for Jenny grew in the days that followed as he watched her set aside her own grief and help the family deal with theirs. She was ready with a soft word, a bracing smile, a shoulder to cry on. He knew she still mourned the loss of Katie, but she grieved privately, crying late at night in her room.

He longed to comfort her, but it was a step in their relationship he was afraid to take.

More and more, he was beginning to understand that Jenny and love were synonymous. And he cursed the past that made him unable to accept what she so freely offered.

For a moment . . . a moment only . . . he wondered if he'd been wrong. Perhaps he could loosen and finally free himself of the shackles of the past. He wished to heaven it were so. But the fear of rejection ran too deep. He didn't dare try.

Unable to sleep one evening, he headed to the kitchen with the intention of finding a snack.

Whimpering caught his attention as he padded barefoot down the hallway. He paused, listening, trying to determine where it had come from. The boys' room. He hesitated, debated about calling Jenny, then knocked lightly.

"Trevor?" he called. "Travis?"

"Who's there?" came a muffled reply.

"David."

"Go 'way."

He was tempted to do just that. What did he know about comforting a crying child? But the soft cries plucked at his heart and brought back childhood memories of being alone and afraid. He waited for a moment longer before the cries gave way to hiccups.

He edged the door open. The room was dark save for the gentle splash of moonlight across the floor, the beds. He let his eyes accustom themselves to the night. A movement in one of the beds caught his attention.

"Whadda you want?" Travis—or was it Trevor?—asked.

"I . . . uh . . . let's go out in the hall. We don't want to wake your brother." Silence met his words.

" 'Kay."

David wondered what he'd been thinking. He swallowed hard as he watched the boy rub red-rimmed eyes. David fumbled for words, hoping he didn't say the wrong thing. He didn't want to embarrass the child, but neither did he want him to feel as if he were alone. Being alone and miserable at nine years old was the most awful thing in the world.

He ought to know. Moved from the one foster home where he'd actually felt wanted, he'd cried himself to sleep more nights than he wanted to remember. Later, he'd learned that tears didn't help. If he cried, it was only in his heart, where it didn't show.

"I . . . uh . . . was on my way to get a snack and wondered if you wanted to join me." He took a stab at the boy's name. "How 'bout it . . . Travis?"

He must have guessed correctly, for Travis nodded slowly. "Yeah. That'd be all right."

Together they walked down the stairs, Travis careful to keep his face turned away.

Hesitating for only a moment, David placed his hand on the boy's shoulder. He felt Travis stiffen and then relax, his acceptance warming David in ways he didn't understand.

In the kitchen, David slathered mustard on thick slices of Jenny's whole-wheat bread, slapped a slab of roast beef between the two pieces, and handed it to Travis. He then proceeded to make a sandwich for himself. They ate in companionable silence, Travis stopping every now and again to blow his nose. David made a point of looking the other way at those times.

He watched the small, flushed face. Travis was working so hard to act as though everything were all right. His valiant effort snagged at David's heart. He understood pride. Maybe too well.

When Travis pushed his plate away, David did the same. He rocked back on his chair and waited, hoping the boy would share his fears.

Travis pleated a paper napkin, his gaze fixed on his task. ''The social worker came today. The same one that came when . . . Katie got 'dopted.''

The words were spoken calmly enough, but David heard the fear behind them. He remembered enough about the foster-care system to understand the significance of a worker's visit. That, coupled with Katie's adoption, was enough to give a little boy nightmares.

He prayed for the right words. ''Do you know what she wanted?''

''She said something about a change in pl . . . placement. That's the word they use when they want to send you somewhere else.'' Travis gulped. ''What if Trevor and I get moved again? Jenny said it wouldn't happen, but what if she's wrong?''

''How many times . . . how many places have you lived?''

''Three. Counting this one. I didn't mind when they pulled us out of the other two. They were crummy. But Jenny's place is special.''

David didn't have to be told that. ''How old were you when . . .'' He couldn't finish the question, but Travis didn't seem to have any problem figuring it out. ''Five. Me and Trevor got put in the first place right before we started kindergarten.''

Five. Hardly more than babies. A year younger than

he'd been when his mother had died and his father had taken off. He pushed the memories aside. Right now, a boy needed his help.

"Did you ask Jenny about what the social worker wanted?"

Travis rubbed his eyes. "I wanted to, but I got scared. Like some baby." Self-disgust dripped from the words, causing David to hide a smile.

"You know, sometimes I get really scared," he said, rubbing his chin.

"You?"

The boy's surprise encouraged David to continue. "Yeah. Me."

Travis's features scrunched together as he thought about it. "I didn't know grown-ups got scared."

"All the time," David confided.

"You're not just saying that?" Travis fixed him with a severe look. "Just 'cause I'm a kid?"

"No way."

"Cross your heart and hope to die?"

"Cross my heart and hope to die." The childhood vow brought back a slew of memories. "Tell you what. How 'bout I talk with Jenny tomorrow? That way I can find out and let you know what's going on."

"That'd be okay, I guess. What . . . what if she says they're gonna move us?"

"Jenny and I'll think of something," he promised. "We won't let anyone take you away." David didn't question his use of the plural. He would find a way to help Travis and Trevor.

"You mean it?" The tentative hope in the boy's voice tugged at David's heart.

"Hey, we're pals, aren't we?"

Travis nodded, and David felt the sweet warmth of friendship.

"That's what pals do, isn't it? Help each other out. Right?"

"Right." Travis spit on his hand before holding it out.

With equal gravity, David did the same. They shook on it.

After Travis was in bed, David headed back to his own room. He had some thinking to do. He'd given a promise, a promise he had no right to make. Now he had to figure out how he was going to keep it.

He knew Jenny well enough to know she wouldn't voluntarily give the boys up, but some things were out of her control. First things first, he reminded himself. First, he needed to find out what the social worker wanted. After that he and Jenny . . .

Since when had he started thinking of him and Jenny as a team? Since the night he'd kissed her? Since the time she'd kissed him back? Impatiently, he shoved the questions from his mind and concentrated on the promise he'd made to a nine-year-old boy.

Only later did it occur to him that he, who'd avoided involvements at all costs, was getting mixed up with the problems of Jenny's family. He sought an excuse—any excuse—and came up with only one. He cared what happened to them. Maybe because of his past. Maybe in spite of it.

Whatever the reason, he cared. Too much.

"Take them away? Where'd he get an idea like that?" Jenny speared her fingers through her hair, pushing it back from her face. The morning sunlight, which had seemed so bright only minutes ago, dimmed for her.

David caught her hand and stilled it, his touch almost succeeding in distracting her. "Travis saw the social worker here yesterday."

Jenny felt a sense of dread fill her. She'd meant to talk to the boys, but something had always gotten in the way. "Miss Baines. Why didn't he ask me?"

"He's scared."

Fool, Jenny berated herself. "Because of Katie."

"Yeah. That's part of it, anyway." He hesitated. "He told me they'd been in a couple of homes before they came here."

Her mouth thinned at the memory of the two wide-eyed little boys who'd appeared at her door. "The wrong kind. Most foster parents are good people, but there're a few that make me . . ." Words failed her. "When Travis and Trevor first came here, I told them they could ask me anything. I never wanted them to be afraid again." Her voice trembled. "I thought after this long, they'd trust me enough—"

"Don't. Don't blame yourself. Travis needs your reassurance, not your guilt." The gentleness in his voice blunted the sting of his words.

He was right. It was easy—too easy—to find escape in guilt rather than deal with a small boy's fears. She looked at David gratefully. "Thanks." She hesitated, not certain he was ready to hear what she wanted to say. "You'd make a good father."

"Yeah, well . . ." He shrugged awkwardly. "That's not my line. It was no big deal."

She'd embarrassed him, she thought, even though she hadn't meant to. But maybe, just maybe, she could jolt him enough to make him realize just how much he had to share with a family.

"You've got one scared kid out there. What say we go find him and put his mind at ease?"

They found Travis under the porch playing with his set of plastic army men.

"How 'bout coming out, seeing as Jenny and I can't come in there?" David asked, hunkering down so that he was at eye level with the boy.

"Please," Jenny added, kneeling beside David.

Travis scooted out. "I guess David told you about last night." Travis's eyes still bore traces of tears, but he angled his chin up. Jenny pulled him closer, laying one arm across his shoulders.

Little-boy pride was a fragile thing, David remembered. He slanted Jenny a look.

"You know, Travis, I was thinking about making this a real family," Jenny began.

Hope filled the boy's eyes.

"If everything goes as planned, I'm going to adopt you and Trevor. That's what Miss Baines was here for yesterday."

"No kidding?"

"No kidding. You and Trevor and I are going to be together forever." She hugged him and was surprised when he let her.

"No one's going to take you away," Jenny promised fiercely. "Not ever." She found her hand nestled in David's and drew strength from it.

"Promise?" Travis asked.

"Promise."

"You hear that, David? Jenny's gonna 'dopt us!"

"I heard."

"If you married Jenny, then you could be our dad. That'd be so cool."

Shock rolled through her as she felt David's grip on her hand go slack. Two baby steps forward, and one giant step back.

Travis looked uncertainly from one to the other. "Wouldn't it?"

"Why don't you go get Trevor?" she suggested, needing a moment to pull her thoughts together. Travis had just put her own hopes and dreams into words— ideas she'd barely dared admit to herself. "Maybe we'll get up a game of ball."

"Can David play too?"

She looked at David, pleased when he nodded. "Sure."

"Yeah!" Travis scampered off.

An awkward silence opened and deepened. It was up to her to break it, Jenny realized.

"I'm sorry. . . ." She gestured vaguely. "Travis didn't mean . . ." Her voice trailed off.

"Yeah. I know."

He sounded as uncomfortable as she felt. But ignoring the problem wasn't going to solve it.

"The boys never knew their father. He took off shortly after they were born. It's only natural they'd want someone in their lives." It wasn't just anyone they wanted, she reminded herself with painful honesty. It was David. Just as she did. But wanting and getting were two different things.

"I'll talk with Travis," she said with as much nonchalance as she could muster. "Explain to him that you and I . . . that we aren't . . ."

David had withdrawn again, gone back into his

shell. "Don't worry. It'll work itself out."

She wasn't so sure about that. Soon he would return to California, and they would get on with their lives. End of story.

But she feared the story wasn't going to have a happy ending. It was hard enough safeguarding her own heart. It was next to impossible to shield those of her children.

"I'm sorry," she said again, standing up and brushing her jeans off.

He let her hand go, almost too willingly. "Right now the important thing is Travis. And Trevor."

Reluctantly, she agreed with him. The tangled mess between her and David would have to wait. "You were great with him."

"Some things you don't forget."

There was pain in his voice, a pain she doubted he was even aware of. "No. I don't guess you do."

He stood and tucked his hands in his pockets, withdrawing from her even more. "Come on. We've got a ball date with a couple of boys."

During the ball game, Trevor peppered Jenny with questions. "Are you really going to adopt us?"

"Yes—"

"When?"

"I don't—"

"Real soon?" Travis asked.

"As soon as possible." She wrapped an arm around each boy. "We're already a family. This'll just make it official."

"Official," Travis repeated, testing the word. "That means like forever, right?"

"Like forever," she repeated, tears glistening in her eyes.

Like forever.

They finished the game, but David couldn't get the words out of his head. He'd never thought of relationships in those terms before. But then, he'd never known a woman like Jenny before.

Jenny and the twins were important to him. He couldn't do much to help with the adoption, but he could make sure her finances were in good shape. That ought to help smooth the way when it came time for the adoption to go through.

With that thought in mind, that evening he looked over the plans he'd drawn up for her business. A spurt of excitement shot through him. The business was small potatoes compared to most of the jobs he dealt with, but the exhilaration he felt at seeing ideas come together was the same, no matter what the scale.

Now he had to convince a banker to catch the same vision.

Chapter Eight

"Mr. Sherwood, Ms. Kirtpatrick." The vice president of the bank rose, gestured for them to be seated, and resettled his considerable bulk in his chair behind the desk. "What can we do for you today?"

Briefly, David laid out the plans for the business.

"You want to sell dried flowers?" The trace of amusement in the man's voice was enough to set Jenny's teeth on edge, but she kept her smile in place.

"Dried flowers and other things," she said with a glance at David. They'd agreed she would be the one to present the specifics of the plan. She pointed to the detailed strategy, complete with projected figures, that David had prepared. "As you can see, the market for naturally grown herbs and related items is increasing. I have the skills and the land. All I need is start-up money."

Mr. Vickers scratched his head. "You've presented a strong case, but a project like this requires more than a little gardening ability and a patch of land. It needs business know-how." He stood, circled the desk, and perched on its edge. ''I've known you for a long time, Jenny. Much as I admire what you're trying to do for those kids, you're no businesswoman.''

She had no answer to that. He was right. In the past she couldn't even balance her own checkbook. Thanks to David, she'd changed. Now all she had to do was convince the banker of that.

''She's got me,'' David said.

Did she? She didn't have a chance to ponder that as Mr. Vickers gave David a speculative look.

''You planning on staying around, maybe helping our girl out?''

Jenny straightened in her chair. She had to be the one to make this work. She couldn't depend on David being around forever . . . however much she might like to.

She chose her words carefully. ''Of course I'm grateful for David . . . Mr. Sherwood's expertise, but this will be my business and I'll be making the decisions.''

Out of the corner of her eye, she caught David's smile of approval.

Mr. Vickers steepled his fingers across his paunch. ''As I said, Jenny, you're not—''

''You've known me for five years. And you know me well enough to know I keep my word. I intend to make this work. With or without your help. If your bank can't help me, I'll go somewhere else.''

She felt David's fingers close around her own. Gratefully, she returned the gentle pressure.

The banker scanned the reports once more. He seemed to come to some kind of decision. ''I think you've got a good plan here, Jenny. What's more, though, I believe in you. I think we can work something out. Provided . . ." He paused, and her heart took a nosedive. "Provided Mr. Sherwood will be staying on as your partner. Temporarily," he added when she would have protested.

She glanced at David, who nodded.

Jenny stood and clasped the banker's outstretched hand. "Thank you. You won't be sorry." Fear of the unknown, elation at the chance to succeed, mingled into a churning mass in her stomach.

"You were something else back there," David said once they were in the car.

Jenny resisted the giddy laugh hovering in her throat. "Thanks. I think." She drew a shaky breath. "What if he'd turned us down?"

"Then we'd have gone to another bank. Just like you told him."

David's confidence helped settle her nerves a little. "Do you think he knew I was bluffing?"

"Were you?"

She didn't need to think about her answer. "No. I'm going to make this work." She reached up to cup his face between her palms, not certain how to thank him. She wanted to kiss him, but he'd been distant since Travis had made his "daddy" statement. Jenny didn't want to chase him completely away. As long as he was still at the house, she had a chance of convincing him to risk his heart. "I owe it all to you."

"Don't thank me yet. Owning your own business is no picnic. By the time you get this off the ground, you may be ready to strangle me."

She already was, but for very different reasons.

"Maybe. Then again, maybe I'll want to do this." She couldn't resist any longer and brushed her lips over his. The quick flash of pleasure in his eyes was enough to make her deepen the kiss. His lips were firm without being hard, soft without being weak. The rightness she felt, the sense of finding what she'd spent a lifetime looking for, filled her with exquisite warmth.

When she eased away from him, he looked bemused. Good, she thought. His kisses had kept her off balance for the better part of a month. It was about time she returned the favor.

"Better watch out," he said softly. "This could become habit-forming."

"For you? Or me?"

"For both of us." As if to prove his point, he drew her into his arms and kissed her until all thoughts of anything else fled her mind. There was only David. And her.

She wasn't naive enough to believe that her love was enough to keep him here forever. Neither was she proud enough to deny herself whatever happiness she found in his arms. It was enough for now.

It had to be.

Starting up a business required more work than she'd ever imagined. At the end of each day, she fell into bed, exhausted but happy. The best part was that the whole family was involved.

She couldn't have done it without David. He had arranged to extend his vacation. He was quietly there, advising, suggesting, but never attempting to take over. For that, as well as a thousand other things, she was grateful.

They made a trip to Denver to register her business name with the state, place advertisements in the various papers, and have cards and letterhead printed.

Her resolve wavered a bit when the bills started coming. "All this money . . . and I haven't sold a thing yet."

"You have to spend money to make money," David reminded her. "You're a businesswoman now, Jenny. It's time to start acting like one."

Her confidence grew as orders began pouring in.

"At this rate, we'll have to hire some more help," Jenny said. The elation and sense of pride she felt was a heady combination.

"Hey, you got us," Trevor said, stuffing a lavender-scented potpourri mixture into lace-trimmed bags.

She rubbed his head. "That's right. But you've got school five days a week."

"I could stay home," he offered, his voice deceptively innocent as he made the suggestion.

"Me too," Travis backed him up. "We wouldn't mind. Honest."

She looked at the identical faces gazing earnestly up at her, and her heart swelled with love. "But I'd mind. Now finish up before you miss the bus."

"How do you manage it?" David asked after she'd seen the boys off.

She looked up from where she was twirling ribbon into a bow before securing it around a sack of potpourri. "Manage what?"

He only smiled. "Never mind. Come on, let's get this order out and then we're going to celebrate."

"I have to finish this." She pointed to the bunches of herbs spread before her. "And then I'm supposed to work on the brochure. I promised the mail-order house I'd have it done by the end of the week. After that—''

"If you don't let up, you're going to collapse. That won't do you or the business any good."

It warmed her that he cared, if only a little bit. "Okay, maybe for a little while."

"This is heavenly," Jenny said, spooning the last of a chocolate mousse into her mouth an hour later.

Getting out with David was just what she needed. They laughed and teased each other like children. And she fell just a bit more in love with him. When the sun lowered in the sky, she found herself reluctant to return home. That had never happened before.

"Thank you for a wonderful day," she said, feeling unaccustomedly shy once they were in the privacy of the car.

He fitted a finger beneath her chin. He was going to kiss her. She knew it. What was more, she wanted it. Wanted it more than she'd wanted anything in a long time.

He lowered his head and slanted his lips over hers. "You're welcome."

David tucked her head against his shoulder. The trip home gave her an opportunity to study him. Light and shadow played across his face. She skimmed her knuckles across his stubbled jaw. He caught her hand and brought it to his lips.

Her skin tingled where his lips left a warm trail of moist kisses, and she struggled to catch her breath.

This day was a memory, to be stored away and taken out when that was all she had.

They reached home all too soon. Reluctant to have their time together end, she turned to him. "You're a nice man, David Sherwood." Before he could deny it, she let herself out and hurried into the house.

"I did it. I contacted the mister again," Mrs. Abernathy, her fuchsia-colored turban slightly askew, announced as Jenny walked inside, followed closely by David.

The romance of the evening faded away when confronted with reality.

Jenny roused herself and threw her arms around the older woman. "That's wonderful. What did he say?"

"He told me that someone I cared about would soon be finding love." She directed a knowing look, first at Jenny and then at David.

Jenny flushed and tried not to dream. The reference was pointed enough to be downright embarrassing. By sheer force of will, she avoided looking at David.

"And then he said he loved me." The old lady's voice cracked on the last three words.

Whatever David felt about communication from beyond the grave, he couldn't deny the real feeling in her voice. He was tempted to reach out and hug her, but his innate reserve stopped him. He also felt a twinge of jealousy—to feel that depth of love even after death was something he didn't dare think about.

Jenny knew no such inhibitions. She slipped an arm around Mrs. Abernathy's shoulders.

"Jenny, you believe the mister talked to me, don't you?" The change in Mrs. Abernathy's voice startled David. She was no longer the brash, wacky, offbeat woman he'd first thought. She was vulnerable and lonely, suddenly looking every bit of her eighty-something years.

"Of course I do. You were married for over forty years. Why wouldn't he try to communicate with you? Love doesn't stop just because you're separated for a while."

"You're right. I don't know why I ever doubted." She kissed Jenny's cheek. "Thank you, dear. You always make me feel so much better."

David waited until she'd departed in a flurry of scarves and incense. "You're something special."

"Mmm?" Jenny gave him an absent look.

"You really love that old lady, don't you?"

She looked surprised that he'd had to ask. "Yes. I do."

"I wish I'd known you sooner, Jenny Kirtpatrick. Things might have been different."

The wistful note in his voice wasn't lost on her.

She put a finger to her lips, surprised to find they were trembling. David had so much to give, but he insisted upon ignoring his feelings.

Her lips firmed into a determined line. He had to accept that he was warm, loving, and giving.

"David, you're a special man. It's time you realized it."

He all but scoffed at her words. "You don't know what you're saying."

"I grew up on stories of knights-errant and fair damsels. I was dreaming of heroes performing courageous deeds while all the other little girls were playing house."

"I'm not a knight in shining armor, Jenny. I'm just a man. And not a very nice one, at that."

"I don't believe you." She leveled her gaze at him and dared him to challenge her. If he wouldn't fight for himself, she'd do it for him.

"Believe it."

She angled her chin at him. "I'm the authority on knights, and I say you are one." She reached up to trace his lips, her fingers lingering there. She felt the tension in him, part of him straining to pull away while the other part yearned to give in to her. Holding her breath, she waited.

"Don't make me into something I'm not, Jenny. It's not fair. To either of us."

When the answer came, she sighed, defeated for the moment. She'd lost the battle. But that didn't mean she was going to lose the war. Reluctantly, she dropped her hand as he pulled away, clearly uncomfortable with her words. "How do you know what's fair to me?"

She saw the confusion in his eyes, a confusion she'd put there. She wouldn't apologize for it. David had so much to give . . . if only she could convince him of it. She reached out, only to drop her hand as the mask slipped over his face. She'd come to recognize it in the weeks David had been here.

Don't. The word was as clear as if he'd uttered it aloud.

Stung, she held her tongue and decided a change of subject was in order. "What do you think about me adopting the boys?"

Clearly relieved that she'd dropped an uncomfortable topic, he stared thoughtfully into the night. "I think it's great. They're good kids. They deserve a real home."

"Miss Baines has already started the paperwork. She promised to push it through as soon as possible."

"What about you being a single parent? I thought the courts usually liked to place kids with couples."

"Trevor and Travis are classified as 'difficult-to-place' because of their age. Most people don't want older kids. They want babies. So I don't think my being a single parent is going to be a problem."

He covered her hand with his own. "They're lucky . . . having you."

"I'm the lucky one."

"Yeah. I guess you are."

Reaching up, she laid her hand against his cheek.

He tipped his head into her caress, turning her palm to his lips before lowering his head. His lips grazed hers, no more than a whisper of a kiss, but it was enough to make her want, want so very much.

If only David recognized his own worth . . . if only she could make him see what she saw every time she looked at him. Not a hero or a knight in shining armor, but simply a man. One who had more to give than he was willing to admit.

It was a hint of a kiss, with only a trace of what existed beyond the barriers he struggled to keep in place. It was all he would permit himself, all he could permit himself. To deepen it, to give in to his feelings as he longed to do, would be to expose the intensity of emotions that he so carefully held in check.

He lifted his head and saw the soft flush that colored her face. If he stayed . . .

The thought caused a frown to skim across his face. Of course he wasn't staying. His life was in California.

His job. His friends. His condo. Each more empty than the last. Each more sterile.

But that didn't mean he was staying here with Jenny and her household. No two people could be more wrong for each other. It wasn't only that they looked at the world from different perspectives; they weren't even looking at the same world.

Jenny looked at her world through rose-colored glasses; if he'd ever been tempted to do the same, David had thrown his glasses away a long time ago.

He looked at the woman who'd so effortlessly made herself part of his life.

"I can't think when I'm around you." The accusation startled him.

"Is that so important?" she asked.

He could hear the smile slipping through her voice despite the pain he'd caused her. It threatened to trigger one of his own. And that he couldn't afford. Not when his very existence depended upon remaining in control. That she could so easily cause him to lose that control was but one more reason to pull back.

"Of course it is—" He stopped. Analyzing, evaluating had been the basis of his life. A very lonely life, he realized. He looked into her eyes and wondered.

He'd spent most of his childhood watching from the sidelines, resigned to being an observer rather than a participant. Observers, he'd learned, didn't attract attention—nor did they get in trouble. That had changed as he'd grown more sure of himself.

Now, he owned one of the largest financial troubleshooting companies in the state. Him, a little kid from nowhere. But it didn't change the loneliness.

Now he could have any woman he wanted—except one.

He burned for her, for Jenny, a woman he could never have.

And for a moment, a very brief moment, he believed that the rest didn't matter. That he was the man she believed him to be, the man she deserved him to be.

The smile was back, a soft, tantalizing curve of her lips.

He gave in to the impulse to brush his hand against Jenny's cheek. Even that brief contact was enough to threaten his resolve. Abruptly, he dropped his hand. Just as abruptly, he turned and walked away. If his legs could have managed it, he would have run.

Jenny stared after him, rubbing her cheek. It was warm where he'd touched her. She concentrated on that, because the rest of her was suddenly cold. So very cold. She hugged herself to ward off the chill. Only, the coldness came from the inside.

David had drawn away from her. Again. It was becoming a pattern. He'd allow himself to get so close and then pull back. Something bleak and heavy settled around her heart with depressing finality. And suddenly, she was too tired to fight him any more.

"David." The word was both a plea and a prayer. She didn't realize she'd spoken aloud until she looked up to find Mrs. Abernathy looking at her, compassion shining from her eyes.

"You love him."

It wasn't a question, and Jenny didn't treat it as such. "Yes."

"I knew it. The moment I laid eyes on him, I knew he was the one for you."

"Did your crystal ball tell you?" If she'd been forewarned, maybe she could have protected herself.

Mrs. Abernathy smiled. "I know I'm a silly old woman, but I know love when I see it."

Jenny returned the smile with a faint one of her own. "He doesn't believe in love. Besides, we're so different from each other. He's programmed his life just like he'd program one of his computers. I believe in taking each day as it comes."

To her surprise, Mrs. Abernathy didn't try to talk her out of her evaluation of their differences. "Did I ever tell you about how I met Mr. Abernathy?"

Puzzled, Jenny shook her head.

"I was telling fortunes in Las Vegas. I was a looker in those days." She patted her hair. "This was red. No henna rinse for me. The mister was a cop, walking a beat. He had the cutest tush. Boy, did he fill out a uniform." She chuckled.

"Anyway, I had my eye on him for a couple of weeks, but he'd never give me the time of day." Mrs. Abernathy paused. "Have I told you this already?"

Jenny barely had time to shake her head again before her friend continued with her story.

"The police were cracking down on what they called scams. The mister walked in just when I was giving a customer a glimpse into the future. When I took the woman's money, he busted me."

"You mean he arrested you?"

"Right down to the handcuffs and reading me my rights. Even frisked me."

"Let me get this straight," Jenny said, torn between

laughter and disbelief. "Your husband arrested you and hauled you off to jail?"

Mrs. Abernathy smiled mischievously. "He wasn't my husband then."

"What happened?"

"He bailed me out. He asked me out the next day, and we started seeing each other. Two weeks later we were married." Her eyes grew dreamy. "In a little chapel on the Strip."

Jenny was beginning to wonder if she'd been had. Mrs. Abernathy had been known to stretch the truth sometimes to make a story better.

"Are you sure—"

"You're wondering if I might be bending the truth a smidgin. Am I right?"

Reluctantly, Jenny nodded, not wanting to doubt this sweet lady.

"I may exaggerate about some things, but never about the mister and me." The old lady's voice cracked on the last words. "We were friends and lovers for almost forty years."

Jenny felt her heart stumble at the emotion in her friend's voice. If only she could find the same for herself. "Why are you telling me all this now?"

Mrs. Abernathy just smiled. "Love doesn't always make sense. It just is. Like the mister and me."

"How do I convince David to give us a chance?"

"Listen to your heart. It won't lead you astray." It sounded so simple.

Jenny managed a smile, though she was no nearer to answering her question than she had been. Her heart screamed that she go after him and tell him that she loved him. Dispassionately, she played out the probable scenario in her mind.

David was a kind man. He'd feel uncomfortable, perhaps even pressured to return the words. As much as she longed to hear them, she couldn't force them. Those words had to be freely given, not out of her need, but his. Until David could say *I love you* and mean it, there was no future for them.

Oh, he was attracted to her. She didn't doubt that. But physical attraction wasn't enough. Not for her. She needed his trust, his respect. Most of all, she needed his love.

For David, love didn't exist. Might never exist.

Chapter Nine

Jenny attacked the pile of orders for Herbs 'n' Stuff. With the business taking off like wildfire, she could barely keep up with the demand for her products.

Another six months and she should be out of debt, with maybe even a little money left over. She spent a few moments entertaining delicious ways of spending it. The idea of having money not already spoken for was a luxury she'd never allowed herself to dream of.

One of the unexpected benefits of the business was that it provided a source of income for her boarders. All three worked part-time, manning the phones and filling orders. The pride in their eyes when they received their paychecks brought tears to Jenny's own.

She owed it all to David. If not for his willingness to act as her temporary partner, the bank would never have agreed to loan her the money she needed. And without his expertise and guidance, she'd never have made it. Her thoughts took her full circle. Back to David.

She knew he couldn't stay here forever. He'd kept

in touch with his office by fax and daily phone calls, but he'd have to return to California soon. She was very much afraid her heart would break when he left. She pushed the thought away and concentrated on what she did have. The present. If it was all she was to have with him, she'd make every minute count.

Her soft sigh was interrupted as gentle hands swept her hair from her neck. A featherlight kiss landed on her nape.

"Mmm." She turned to meet David's lips with her own.

"You like that?"

"What do you think?"

"I think you're beautiful. I also think you need a day off."

"Maybe next week—"

"That's what you said last week. When was the last time you played hooky? Come on," he said, taking the order slips from her and pulling her up. He pushed open the door. "How often do we get a day like today?"

She followed him and inhaled deeply, savoring the crisp breeze.

Seduced by both the golden day and the appeal she read in his eyes, she slipped her hand in his. "Okay."

David seemed more relaxed, more at ease with himself. And with her. Perhaps this was his way of telling her . . . what? She wouldn't spoil the day by analyzing it to death. Today was an unexpected gift. And she intended to treat it as such.

He took her to an estate sale, where she happily poked through piles of treasures. "How did you know I'd like this?"

"I noticed your paper turned to the classified ads and saw where you'd circled some sales. You really like this sort of thing?" he asked as she sorted through piles of treasures.

She nodded. "Someone once loved these things. I can't bear to see them sold like so much junk by people who don't care about them or the past."

Her happiness deflated a bit when she caught David looking at her oddly, as if he had something to tell her and didn't know how. A moment later, she decided she must have imagined it, for he gave her a lopsided smile that warmed her inside and out.

The day was dipped in color. Reds and browns. Greens and golds. Blues and mauves. If she were an artist, she'd find a way to capture them on canvas.

A tiny frown worked its way between her brows as she remembered the paints she'd given David for his birthday. So far she hadn't seen him use them. Maybe soon. After the magic they'd shared today, she was ready to believe anything was possible. Maybe even love.

"Thank you for today," she said softly when they returned home.

He pressed a kiss to her palm and tucked her against him. "No. Thank you."

Content, she leaned against him. Love, hot and sweet, welled up inside her. Emboldened by what she saw in his eyes, she took a chance and said what was in her heart. "I love you."

She felt, more than heard, his sharp intake of breath.

Slowly, she turned in his arms, needing to see his face. "I love you, David." She waited, hoping, praying.

He lifted his hand to brush her hair back from her face. "I care about you, Jenny. You know that."

She nodded, her hopes beginning to crumble.

"I care about you more than I ever dreamed possible."

"I know that. I feel it." She placed her hand on her heart. "Here."

He took her hand and cradled it within his own. "Jenny . . ."

She heard the hitch in his breath, the husky note in his voice that told her everything she wanted to know. She wouldn't allow herself to think about failure.

"You love me." She laced her arms around his neck and lifted her face for a kiss. "I know you love me."

Gently, he freed himself, and she felt the loss of his touch. "Jenny, I care about you. I need you. I want you. You have to believe me. I've never said those things to another woman."

Moved by the rough emotion in his voice, she said, "I know that." In vain, she waited for the words she needed to hear.

"I'm trying to be totally honest with you."

A frown puckered her brow as her natural optimism slipped. "I don't understand."

"I'd do anything for you. You know that, don't you?"

She nodded, still puzzled.

"Anything, but . . ."

She was beginning to understand. "Anything but say you love me. Is that it?"

His silence confirmed her guess.

"But today . . ."

"I wanted to have one last day with you, make one more memory."

"So today was your way of telling me good-bye."

He nodded. "I'm leaving tomorrow."

"Because of what I said?"

"Because of what I *can't* say."

Her laugh came out as a strangled sob as her hopes and dreams died. "You know what's funny? You already love me. I see it in your eyes. I feel it whenever you touch me. But you can't say the words. You can't force yourself to say the words, because if you did, you'd be vulnerable like the rest of us. And that's the one thing you can't be, the one thing you won't let yourself be."

"That's what keeps me alive."

"No. That's what keeps you alone." She started to pull away and then stopped. "I love you, David. I always will. Nothing's going to change that. Not even you."

Her heart contracted as she watched the shutter come over his eyes.

"I'm not going to apologize for loving you. Or for my feelings. I'm not asking for anything but that you believe me when I say I love you." When he remained silent, she shook her head. "But even that's too much, isn't it?"

He should have seen it coming. And he had. He just hadn't wanted to acknowledge it. Jenny was a romantic, believing in the basic goodness of people. In his case, that belief was definitely misplaced. Greedily, he'd accepted her friendship, basking in her sweetness, soaking up the warmth she gave to anyone who entered the magic circle she spun around her.

Now it was time to pay up. That it was ripping the soul from him was only right. He deserved that and more. Somewhere his subconscious registered the opening and closing of the car door.

He looked up to find himself alone. This time it had been Jenny who'd walked away. Who could blame her? She'd laid her heart bare, offering him the most precious gift a man could desire. And what did he do? Threw it back in her face.

Part of him longed to accept what she offered, to believe in the magic of love. But the part of him honed by pain and loneliness rejected the idea of love. At least for him.

A soft, clear whistle drew his attention outside. Unable to help himself, he followed the sound. He searched the porch and yard but found nothing. Fairies, Jenny would tell him.

Heaven help him, he was afraid if he stayed here much longer he'd start believing in them himself. And, if he believed in fairies, he might even come to believe in love.

At least he could leave her with her finances in order. Back in his room, he spent the evening at the computer, updating the bookkeeping and entering projected sales figures. The business had taken off beyond his wildest dreams. If it kept up at this rate, Jenny would have no more money worries.

He found Jenny in the garden the following morning. For once, her hands were still as she sat cross-legged on the ground. The temptation simply to look at her undermined his resolve to do what he had to.

"I like the mountains this way," she said. "They look at peace."

He was no longer surprised at her uncanny ability to sense his presence. Nor did he question her observation on the mountains. No tourist-trite descriptions of *majestic, snowcapped*, or *beautiful* for Jenny. She saw peace.

For a moment, he wanted that for himself. He wanted to be able to see the world through Jenny's eyes. And he knew he couldn't. He would end up tainting all that set her apart from him.

He hurt all over. A bone-deep hurt that had nothing to do with the sunburn he'd gotten yesterday while they attended the sale, and everything to do with what he saw in Jenny's eyes.

He found refuge in brusqueness. "Everything's set up at the bank. Mr. Vickers has agreed to give you the extension as long as you keep up the payments. With the business taking off like it has, you shouldn't have any problem. If you do, give me a call."

"Thank you, but I don't think that'll be necessary."

He ignored the small stab of hurt and pressed on. "The new brochures ought to be arriving in the next week or two. Once they do, mail them out. I left a mailing list on the computer. All you need—"

"You've gone over this already," she pointed out gently.

He was stalling. He knew it. Anything to postpone saying what he knew needed to be said. His brain scrambled for something else, something he'd forgotten to tell her, anything to avoid the inevitable.

"I'm leaving today." The words sounded unnaturally loud to his ears.

He let his gaze find hers. Her eyes held no surprise, only a heart-splintering sadness.

How could he leave this woman? For the first time in his life he didn't doubt the existence of love. He doubted only his ability to give it in return.

"I love you," she said simply.

They were the most humbling words a man could hear. If only he were the right man . . . For a moment, he was tempted to stay. Maybe he could— As swiftly as the thought formed, he rejected it. Jenny deserved more than his feeble attempts at trying to return her love.

"I'll be out of here by today."

"You said that."

"Yeah. I guess I did."

He waited for the words of reproach, words he deserved to hear, but there were none. "I already said good-bye to the others."

"They'll miss you. The boys especially."

"I'll miss them. They're good kids. I hope everything goes all right with the adoption."

"Thanks."

"If things were different . . ." He let the words trail off because he knew it wasn't *things* that needed to be different. It was him.

"Go," she said, her voice so soft it reached him only because he strained to hear it. "Run away."

"That's not fair."

"Maybe not. But it's true. You're running away from love. A word you can't even say."

He wanted to argue with her. He wasn't running away. He'd never run from anything in his life. But arguments had no place in good-byes. "Jenny . . ." He knew if he reached for her, his hands would tremble, so great was his need to touch her. He wanted her with a longing so acute that it was a physical ache. And he knew he couldn't have her.

"Please. I don't think I can stand much more." A tear squeezed out of the corner of her eye.

He caught it on the tip of his finger and watched as it dissolved at his touch, as ephemeral as the morning dew. Like his chance for happiness? He dismissed the idea as fanciful.

"Jenny . . ."

The tears were coming faster now. They trickled unchecked down her cheeks, glistening against her skin.

Her tears, as always, stopped him. He had no weapons against them. He thought about trying to touch her once more and rejected the idea, whether for her sake or his, he wasn't sure.

He paused. "I wish . . ."

"I know."

The steadiness of her voice shamed him. Even now, she was the strong one.

"Good-bye, Jenny," he said, knowing he was saying good-bye to more than her. He was saying good-bye to the only true happiness he'd ever known.

"Good-bye, David."

Hearts do not really break, Jenny decided. *They may get bruised. Or cracked. But they don't break.* She was living proof of it. If her heart were really broken, she wouldn't be able to feel.

Right now, she felt too much. All of it pain.

* * *

The next day it rained. Jenny lay alone in the four-poster bed, the bed she'd never shared, and listened to the dance of the rain as it tapped against the window.

She welcomed the ashen sky. Perhaps the grayness of the day would mask the pain in her eyes, a pain makeup had failed to cover. She showered and dressed and then started toward the kitchen. David was gone, but the rest of the family still needed breakfast.

Comfortable smells and sounds filled the old house. The creaking of pipes as someone turned on the water, the aroma of freshly brewed coffee, the boys' voices raised in what promised to be a humdinger of a fight. As if to reinforce that prediction, a yell blared from the kitchen.

Despite the pain that squeezed her heart, she smiled faintly, thinking of her family. One thing was certain: she'd never be bored around here. With a small sigh, she quickened her pace. The scene that greeted her wasn't anything out of the ordinary. Puddles of milk and cereal covered the floor, table, and chairs.

"Jenny, Trevor knocked over my cereal," Travis said in an aggrieved voice.

"He called me a nerdhead," Trevor defended himself.

Something inside her snapped. Anger, fresh and hot, felt good. She gave in to it.

"Trevor, get the mop and clean this up. Travis, you help him." When they failed to move, she said, "Now."

The shrill tone of her voice had the twins turning to stare at her. She was aware of her boarders' shock, surprise then concern written plainly on their faces.

Obviously, she'd stunned them as much as she had the boys.

"You hollered at us," Travis said, sounding more awed than scared.

"Real loud," Trevor added.

She flushed. She never yelled at the boys. Never. They'd heard enough yelling in their lives already. "I'm sorry. I didn't mean to scream at you."

"It's okay, Jenny," Trevor said in a small voice. "I'm sorry for spilling Travis's cereal."

"Me too," Travis said. "I'm sorry for calling Trevor a nerdhead."

Their swift forgiveness warmed her heart even as it deepened her shame. She brushed a kiss across their foreheads. "I guess we're all a little on edge."

"It's 'cause David's gone," Travis said.

The innocent words hit her like a blow to the gut. For a moment, she felt the room spinning by her. A deep breath restored enough of her composure to enable her to speak calmly. "That's right. David's gone. We're going to miss him." She was proud of her matter-of-fact voice. She let her gaze stray to the window. A bit of sunshine tried to work its way through the cloud-laden sky.

"He gave me this." Travis held out a baseball mitt.

"He gave me one too," Trevor said. "He said he couldn't be here for our birthday, so he was giving them to us early."

A fresh wave of pain hit her as she remembered the shopping trip, when they'd picked out the mitts together.

"Why'd you send him away?" Travis asked.

"I didn't—"

"Okay, everybody out," Mrs. Abernathy said. She shooed the two elderly men and the boys out.

Jenny sank onto a chair, uncaring of the cereal and milk smeared on it. She cradled her head in her palms. The pain couldn't last forever, she assured herself. No more than fifty or sixty years at the most.

She was still there when Mrs. Abernathy returned a few minutes later. She quietly began cleaning up the mess, stirring Jenny to action.

"I'll do that."

"I thought you might." Looking pleased with herself, Mrs. Abernathy wiped off a chair and sank onto it.

"I think I've been had."

Mrs. Abernathy looked at her, an innocent expression in her eyes. "Oh?"

Jenny finished wiping off the table and floor. "Yeah." She hugged her friend. "Thanks. I owe you one."

"Trevor was right, you know. About David."

Not that again. "I didn't send him—"

"I know that. But you didn't stop him."

"How could I?"

"A woman has her ways."

The words sounded like something straight from an old movie. Jenny pressed her fingers to her lips, not certain whether it was to stifle a hysterical desire to laugh or the sob that was perilously close.

"What was I supposed to do? Hog-tie him?"

"If that's what it takes." The old lady pressed her hand. "Go after him, child."

"He doesn't want me."

"That boy doesn't know what he wants. That doesn't mean he doesn't love you."

"He doesn't believe in love."

Mrs. Abernathy snorted. "Most men don't. Not even when it's right under their noses." Her voice gentled. "He needs you."

"How do you know?"

"His eyes were cold when he came here. Now they're alive."

"How did you get so wise?" Jenny asked, wanting to believe her friend and not daring to let herself.

A booming laugh rang out. "When you've lived as many years as I have, you learn a few things along the way."

Jenny gave her best smile and knew it was a wasted effort. "I have to work this out for myself."

"You'd know best," Mrs. Abernathy said in the tone of one who clearly believed just the opposite.

Jenny turned an exasperated look on her. Great. Just great. Far from getting any sympathy, she was labeled the bad guy of the piece.

Right now, she wanted nothing more than to crawl back to her room and bawl her eyes out. Her shoulders straightened. She refused to give in to the misery. If she did, she might never find her way out of it. Maybe a walk would clear her mind.

The morning's patchy layer of clouds had sealed over, erasing the hint of sunshine she'd glimpsed earlier. Her sneakered feet squeaked as she walked across the lawn toward her herb garden.

Heedless of the mud, she sank onto the ground. Lifting a stalk of lavender, she bent her head to sniff it.

The sweet fragrance it released took her back to the day David had come into her life.

Was it then she'd started falling in love with him? Like a movie slowly flickering to life, her memory stirred, and image upon image appeared. Had it been the first time he'd kissed her? Maybe it had happened when she'd cried in his arms upon learning that Katie would be taken away.

Impatient with her musings, she closed her eyes, willing the pictures away. It didn't matter when it had happened. Or how. Or why. She'd fallen in love with him. Period.

The days dragged into a week.

Passed was too kind a word for her day-by-day struggle to simply function, Jenny decided, dragging herself from bed. Thank goodness for her family. At least with the demands of caring for them, she had little opportunity to dwell on her misery.

A guilty flush spread across her cheeks. She'd given them less than her best the past week. Not that she hadn't performed the necessary things, it was just that her heart hadn't been in them. It had been otherwise occupied.

Well, that was going to change. Starting today.

Maybe she'd make an extra-special breakfast—waffles, sausage, orange juice. She coerced her lips into a semblance of a smile and headed downstairs. It was a poor imitation of her usual, but it was an attempt.

"You feeling all right, Jenny?" Mrs. Abernathy asked, taking her hand.

Jenny's smile grew more determined. "Fine."

"You sure? You're looking a mite peaked." She

turned Jenny's palm over. "I could read your palm. See what the future has in store for you."

"I'm fine." Gently, Jenny freed her hand. "How do blueberry waffles sound?"

"Awesome," Trevor said, walking into the kitchen.

Mrs. Abernathy smiled. "I guess that answers your question."

Jenny started mixing the batter, then poured it into the waffle iron. She placed sausage in a skillet. It sizzled, releasing a spicy aroma.

"Something up?" Mr. Ambrose wandered in, sniffing appreciatively.

"Jenny's making waffles," Trevor said.

"What's the occasion?"

Jenny felt her good intentions fade; doggedly, she held on to them. Her plans for a special breakfast had aroused questions she'd rather not answer. "Nothing." Realizing how abrupt she must have sounded, she softened the word with another smile, this one almost genuine.

She raised her head in time to observe the speculative looks traded between Mr. Ambrose and Mrs. Abernathy.

"I'll set the table," he volunteered.

It was then that Jenny knew how bad she really looked. Mr. Ambrose had never set the table before. "Thanks."

Within minutes, she had breakfast on the table and her smile in place. Family talk centered around the upcoming school carnival.

After making impressive inroads on his waffles and sausage, Trevor turned his attention toward Jenny. "David's been gone a week."

Calmly, she wiped her mouth and laid down her fork. "That's right."

"When's he coming back?"

"He's not." *He's not. He's not. He's not.* The words echoed through her brain so that she almost missed the boy's trembling lips.

"Not ever?"

Travis looked up for the first time. "Never?"

"I'm afraid not." She longed to comfort them, to tell them David's absence was only temporary, but she'd vowed never to lie to the children, no matter how painful the truth might prove. The truth in this case was just about as bad as it got.

She pushed her chair from the table and stood. "Time to get ready for school."

The twins started to grumble, looked at each other, and shrugged.

"I'll clean up," Mr. Ambrose volunteered.

Jenny shook her head, grateful for the offer but unwilling to accept. Selfishly, she wanted to hold on to the small chores of living, the homey acts that enabled her to keep her sanity. "I can do it. But thank you." She pressed a kiss to his cheek and smiled when a blush crept up his neck.

After straightening the kitchen and seeing the boys off, she found herself at loose ends.

"You didn't sleep much last night, did you?" Mrs. Abernathy asked. "Or any other night for the last week."

Jenny thought about denying it and knew the evidence was there on her face, in her eyes. "No."

"Go after him, honey. It's not just him who needs you. You need him too. We all do."

Jenny knew her friend was only speaking the truth, but the words hurt. A dull ache settled around her heart. "Thanks for caring. But I can't run after him. If David wants me, he knows where to find me."

"Are you sure . . . ?"

"I'm sure," Jenny said firmly, wishing she believed it.

A disapproving sigh escaped Mrs. Abernathy's lips. "You'd know best," she said, the tone, if not the words, a gentle rebuke.

By noon, Jenny wasn't so sure of that.

A call from the school principal had her rushing to the school. The principal, an old friend, gave her a sympathetic smile before ushering her into his office, where she found the two culprits.

"Okay, give," she said, fixing her gaze on first one twin and then the other.

The story came out in bits and pieces, with only occasional corrections from the principal.

"You put the female rabbit in the cage with the male?" Jenny asked, wanting to make sure she understood.

"We just wanted to see what would happen," Trevor said.

They should know in about four weeks, she thought. "What're you going to do with these two?" she asked the principal.

"I think a week of staying after school ought to do it."

She thanked him, gave the boys her best you'd-better-behave-or-else look, and then, unable to help herself, kissed them.

By the time she returned home, she was exhausted and certain that the day couldn't get any worse.

She was wrong.

Chapter Ten

The washer stopped. Totally, completely stopped. As in never-to-run-again stopped. As in where-was-she-going-to-find-the-money-to-buy-a-new-one   stopped. As in . . .

"Jenny," Mrs. Abernathy said. "There's water on the floor."

Jenny looked down, only now noticing that the toes of her sneakers were wet. "Great." She turned off the main water valve. In a few months, she might have enough money put away to buy a new one, but what was she going to do until then?

What else could go wrong?

She answered her own question as she opened the lid to the washer. A tub full of sudsy water and sopping clothes awaited her.

Two hours later, her arms aching from rinsing and wringing out clothes by hand, she hung the last pair of jeans on the line.

"I swear, those boys go through more clothes than

six children ought to,'' Mrs. Abernathy said, handing
Jenny a clothespin.

''Don't I know it,'' she said without turning around.
''Thanks for helping.''

''You're welcome, honey.'' The older woman
huffed a bit as she made her way to the porch and
settled on the swing.

Jenny shoved the rest of the clothespins back in the
basket and hurried over to sit by her friend. She should
never have permitted Mrs. Abernathy to stand out in
the sun hanging up clothes. Her face was unnaturally
flushed; her breath came in sharp puffs.

''Are you all right?''

''Just have to catch my breath.'' Mrs. Abernathy
gave an annoyed sigh. ''Getting old's the pits. Time
was I could do twenty loads and not raise a sweat
when I worked in the laundry in Vegas. After I married the mister, I gave up telling fortunes. It didn't
look good, him being on the force and all.''

Mrs. Abernathy's breathing had slowed, and Jenny
sighed in relief. If anything happened to her friend . . .
She shivered at the thought. ''Let's go inside. You can
lie down and—''

''Not yet. I have something to tell you,'' Mrs. Abernathy said, sounding unaccustomedly nervous. ''I
wanted to wait, what with you feeling so down and
all, but as Mr. Ambrose said, at our age, we don't have
time to be waiting.''

Jenny's brows pinched together as she tried to follow the convoluted sentence. ''Wait for what?''

''Mr. Ambrose has asked me to marry him.'' A
pretty blush stained the wrinkled face.

Of course. The guilty looks they exchanged when

she saw them holding hands. The way Mrs. Abernathy's eyes lit up when Mr. Ambrose walked into a
room. His new energy and enthusiasm for life. If she
hadn't been so caught up in her own misery, she'd
have seen the signs.

"I'm so happy for you." Jenny gave her friend a
quick hug.

"I hoped you'd feel that way."

"Why wouldn't I . . . ?" Realization came, and with
it, a flash of shame as jealousy registered. "I've been
pretty wrapped up in myself lately, haven't I?"

"Just a bit." The old woman's smile softened any
possible sting in the words.

"I'm sorry."

"Hush. You've got no call to feel sorry. You're
hurting. And heartache's the worst kind of hurt there
is."

Jenny blinked back tears at the compassion in the
words.

Tears formed in Mrs. Abernathy's eyes as well.
"Look at us. Blubbering away like a couple of water-
ing pots."

Jenny managed a smile. "No more tears," she
promised. "Except happy ones."

"That David ought to be horsewhipped," Mrs. Abernathy said, her fierce scowl comical on her usually
serene face.

Jenny held up a hand. "David's out of the picture.
Besides," she added with a trace of a smile, "we're
talking about your love life. Not mine." Hers didn't
exist.

Mrs. Abernathy blushed again. "I've talked to the
mister about this. He's given us his blessing."

"You talked to Mr. Abernathy about marrying Mr. Ambrose?"

"Of course. I couldn't make a decision like this without talking it over with him."

"Of course not."

"I've been talking with him for the last eight years, and I intend to go right on doing so. Henry"—she blushed at the use of her fiancé's given name—"understands." She hesitated. "Do you think we're silly old fools? Marrying at our age?"

The two oldsters showed more sense than she and David had. "Do you love him?"

"With all my heart, and he loves me."

A pang of envy shot through Jenny. She squelched it as best she could. "I think it's wonderful. Have you decided when?"

"As soon as we can arrange it. As Henry says, at our age, we don't have time to waste."

"Would you like to have it here?"

"Nothing would make us happier. You know neither of us have any family outside of you and the kids. I was hoping you'd be my maid of honor."

Setting aside her own pain, Jenny was determined to make this the best wedding possible. "I'd love to. We can decorate the living room and—"

"We were thinking of having it outside. What do you think of a garden wedding?"

"I think it sounds beautiful," Jenny said, a hitch in her voice. And heart.

They spent the next hour making plans. Jenny's earlier sadness melted away as she rejoiced in her friend's happiness, and her bruised heart felt better than it had since David had left.

* * *

"What can we do?" Trevor asked when they told the rest of the family.

"You two can be ushers," Mrs. Abernathy said.

"What's an usher?" Travis asked.

"He sees people to their chairs," Jenny said.

"Can't they see the chairs by themselves?"

"It's not . . ." Jenny looked at Mrs. Abernathy and Mr. Ambrose, who only chuckled.

"It's part of the nonsense people do at weddings," Mr. Ambrose said. "Womenfolk like to do things up fancy."

Travis made a face. "Oh. Girl stuff."

Trevor rolled his eyes.

"Ushers are a very important part of the ceremony," Mrs. Abernathy said, directing a stern look at her fiancé.

Mr. Ambrose turned innocent eyes on her. "Did I say something wrong?"

"Not a thing, dear," Mrs. Abernathy said sweetly. "We'll just let you tell the boys about the suits."

Jenny chuckled at his chagrined expression. She and Mrs. Abernathy retreated to the living room to discuss color schemes, leaving him to explain to the boys why they had to wear Sunday clothes in the middle of the week.

Talk of the wedding occupied the family for the next several days. Jenny found herself alone with the twins one evening when the engaged couple went to shop for rings and Mr. Zwiebel went to bed early.

"Jenny, I've been thinking," Travis said.

Something in his tone caused her to put down the

sock she was darning and look at him. "What is it, honey?"

"When Mr. Ambrose and Mrs. Abernathy get married, where will they live?" A frown creased his face.

Jenny knew what he was worrying about. First Katie had gone away. And now maybe two more members of the family were leaving also.

"Will they live here?" Trevor asked. "They're like our grandparents."

"I don't know," she said honestly. "I don't want them to leave, but sometimes we have to let people go."

"Like you did when David went away?"

The gut-punch jolt she felt upon hearing David's name hadn't lessened over the last two weeks. "Something like that," she said at last.

"Oh."

The two identical faces fell, their small features pinched with pain.

"We love them," Trevor said.

"I know, sweetheart. That means we'll be happy for them wherever they decide to live. Right?"

"Right," Travis said.

"Right," Trevor echoed.

After the boys had gone to bed and Mr. Ambrose and Mrs. Abernathy had returned, Jenny broached the subject to the engaged couple.

"We'd like to stay right here, if it's all right with you," Mrs. Abernathy said. "This is our home."

"We'd never leave you," Mr. Ambrose added.

Jenny didn't bother to hide her tears. "Maybe we could knock down a wall between the bedrooms and make them into one large room," Jenny said, thinking out loud. "Maybe even put in a bathroom."

"That sounds wonderful. We've been wondering how we'd manage the two of us in one room," Mrs. Abernathy admitted.

"Didn't worry me," her fiancé said, his eyes sparkling with mischief. "All we need's a bed. It doesn't even have to be a big one, since we'll be cuddling up close."

The blush that stained Mrs. Abernathy's face made her look like a young girl, Jenny reflected. She felt a pang of envy, which she promptly pushed away. The two of them deserved every bit of happiness they could find. Despite her resolve to be happy, though, the feeling persisted.

She felt completely alone. The house was full of people. They tiptoed around her, treating her like an invalid. Their sensitivity only served to depress her further. She needed time to heal, solitude, and—she winced as a yell pierced the air—silence. A rare commodity around here.

Still, it was home. And she wouldn't trade it for all the solitude and silence in the world.

Home.
Not by any stretch of the imagination could his condo be called home, David thought. It was shelter. Comfortable, even lavish shelter. But shelter nonetheless.

He let his gaze take in the professionally decorated living room. It was immaculate, thanks to the efforts of his housekeeper. It was also as cold as the breeze that whipped across the ocean at night.

When he'd purchased the condo five years ago, it

fit all his requirements. Close to the ocean. Spectacular view. Contemporary design and layout.

Now he moved about the room restlessly. His footprints left tracks across the just-vacuumed carpet, the only sign that somebody did indeed live there.

He opened a magazine, gave it a cursory glance, and left it on the glass coffee table. Deliberately, he rumpled a sofa cushion. The wrinkles dissolved even as he watched, as though trained to straighten themselves.

He wandered over to the window and swiped a finger against the sill. No hint of dust clung to it. Irrationally, the realization annoyed him. Even dust couldn't survive the sterile environment he'd chosen to call home.

There was that word again.

Home.

It wasn't like Jenny's house, where clutter and love mixed together in equal parts. Not for the first time did he find himself missing her . . . and the colorful chaos that comprised her household. Who'd have thought that he'd miss something as simple and uncomplicated as the companionship of those people, people who'd accepted a loner like him and made him part of their lives?

He missed them all. Trevor and Travis. Mr. Ambrose and Mr. Zwiebel and Mrs. Abernathy. Ralph and Daphne and Ginger and Sheila. And Jenny. The heart and soul of the chaotic household that was more of a home than the antiseptic rooms of his condo could ever be.

It all came back to Jenny.

Once again, he wondered what would have happened if he'd stayed. He'd spent years building fences around himself, making sure he didn't get too close to anyone, that he didn't open himself up to that kind of hurt by being vulnerable.

And then he'd met Jenny, and she didn't seem to notice the fences, or, if she did, she chose to ignore them. Suddenly, he found himself living in a world of colors and sounds and feelings. Did she have any idea what she'd done? Did she know she'd dragged him out of his shell and into the world?

For a moment . . . only a moment . . . he indulged in a fantasy of Jenny and him together. The fantasy dissolved as reality hit him. What did he know about commitment? Or permanency? Or loving and cherishing a woman?

Nothing.

He wasn't the right man for her. Someday, she'd understand that and appreciate the fact that he'd had the good sense to get out of her life before he destroyed the love she'd offered him. She'd get over him eventually and find someone who'd love her as she deserved to be loved. A mirthless smile tightened his lips. Probably a lot sooner than he liked to contemplate. She was too lovely, too giving to stay alone for long.

She'd find someone else, all right. Someone who could give her everything she deserved. Someone who wasn't scarred by the past . . . someone who knew how to love.

If he were any kind of a man, he'd be happy for her when it happened. And he would be, he promised himself fiercely. Even if it killed him.

Work was the best antidote, and he threw himself

into it with a vengeance. Contrary to his stated policy, where he accepted only select jobs, he issued a directive that the firm was to take every job offered. Then he personally oversaw each of them, refusing to delegate even the smallest detail.

His temper, always even until now, erupted over minor matters. His staff began avoiding him. If he wasn't careful, he'd end up all alone at work. Just as he was in his personal life.

He hadn't been able to bring himself to get rid of the art supplies Jenny had given him for his birthday. He'd stashed them in a closet upon his return to California. It was crazy. The last time he'd lifted a paintbrush had been over twenty years ago.

He'd throw them out. They were just taking up space. He reached for them, fully intending to haul them to the trash can, but his hands lingered on the brushes. Sable. Jenny had bought him the best, even though she could ill afford it.

Two hours later, he surveyed his sketch with a critical eye. Something was wrong. The features were right. But they lacked the sparkle, the spirit that was uniquely Jenny. After working for another hour, he stepped back. It still wasn't right, but it came closer to capturing her essence.

Over the next week, he worked and reworked the sketch until he was satisfied. Then came translating it into oils. He didn't question his drive to finish the portrait, but kept at it with a dogged determination that he'd reserved for work up until now.

A consulting job with an East Coast firm required he leave first thing the next morning. When he arrived home and saw the letter bearing a Colorado postmark on his desk, he pounced on it. The childish scrawl on the letter baffled him.

He ripped open the envelope. His gaze dropped to the bottom of the page. Travis.

"...and the washer quit. Jenny says it's dead. I didn't know machines died, did you? Anyway, me and Trevor miss you a lot. Can you come visit us sometime? Maybe you could come out for the wedding."

Wedding?

He read the letter through again, hoping he'd made a mistake. Whose wedding? Jealousy surged through him before he remembered that he had no rights where Jenny was concerned. None at all.

He wadded the paper into a ball before thinking better of it and smoothing out the wrinkles. However tenuous it was, it was his only link to Jenny. A ridge formed between his brows as he remembered the amount of laundry that Jenny's family generated in a week. Running a business gave her no time to deal with a recalcitrant washing machine. A smile nipped at his lips as he thumbed through the Yellow Pages and then picked up the phone.

For a moment, he questioned what he was about to do. If Jenny was getting married, her fiancé might resent David's interference. In the end, he let his heart have its way.

He then wandered out to the balcony of his condominium. Stars winked; the moon played hide-and-seek behind a cloud. Amethyst shadows dimpled the pocket-sized yard. The ocean stretched beyond, a deeper black than the sky.

He found no pleasure in the view, as he once had. Perhaps if he were sharing it, he might recapture the sense of peace he'd once felt upon seeing the miles of uninterrupted water.

Twilight dwindled into evening, evening into the empty hours of the night. He barely repressed a shudder. Nights held their own special kind of misery, a loneliness so acute that it was a palpable thing.

A breeze stirred. He listened, waiting. For what? *The fairies.* The answer came so swiftly that he winced. *You're losing it, man. And all because of one slightly crazy woman who's turned you inside out.*

Jenny. Always Jenny. He stalked back inside.

Scanning the latest printout of a company's profit-and-loss statement, he found his mind wandering. What was Jenny doing right now? With Jenny, you never knew. She could be constructing another volcano or holding a séance with Mrs. Abernathy. A smile touched his lips. He never thought he'd miss the old lady, with her turbans and jewels and off-the-wall predictions. But he did.

Truth was, he missed Jenny's whole wacky household. They had accepted him without question. It was the same with Jenny. He didn't have to prove anything to her. All he had to do was love her. And accept her love in return.

And therein lay the problem.

Chapter Eleven

The delivery arrived just as Jenny slipped into a steaming bath, hoping to soak away the morning's frustrations.

The boys had whined their way through breakfast and dawdled in getting ready for school until they'd missed the bus. She'd driven them to school, ignoring their sulks and pouts.

Her sigh of pleasure was barely a memory when the knock sounded at the door. She sank further into the tub of scented water. Maybe if she ignored it, whoever it was would go away.

"Jenny?"

This time her sigh was one of frustration. All she'd wanted was to grab a few minutes for herself.

"Jenny," Mr. Ambrose called through the door. "Delivery for you."

"Could you deal with it?" she yelled back.

" 'Fraid not. The man says he needs your signature."

She rose out of the water regretfully, watching as

171

the bubbles popped one by one. "Just a minute." She toweled off and tied her robe around her.

Downstairs, she was still blotting her hair dry. "Okay. What's so important that it couldn't wait for ten minutes?"

"This." Mr. Ambrose gestured toward the front door.

A man in a blue service uniform slouched against the doorjamb. "Washer and dryer, ma'am. Where do you want 'em?"

She looked past him to the yard, where two large cardboard boxes sat. "There's been a mistake. I didn't order these."

"Got the purchase order right here," he said, shoving a form under her nose.

She scanned it before thrusting it back to him. "Look, I didn't buy anything. Would you please take them back where they came from?"

He pulled a red handkerchief from his pocket and wiped the sweat from his neck. "Can't."

"But—"

"Lady," he said in a long-suffering voice. "I can leave 'em in the yard or take 'em inside. Your choice."

She couldn't let him leave expensive appliances in the middle of her yard. Not with the sky threatening rain. "Take them to kitchen, around back."

He gave her an approving smile. "Now you're talking."

She scrambled up the stairs, pulled on jeans and a sweatshirt, and hurried back down just as he was wheeling a huge box through the kitchen door.

"Where do you want 'em?" he asked.

With her old washer occupying the corner, she had no choice but to point to the middle of the kitchen floor.

He gave her a doubtful look. "You sure? I got orders to hook these up and get rid of the old one."

"But I'm not going to keep—"

"Lady, this here washer and dryer are bought and paid for. You gotta keep 'em. Now, where'd you want 'em?"

"I . . . uh . . ."

"Lady, I got other deliveries to make today. You planning on keeping me here all day?"

Frustrated, she motioned to the corner. "There. What about the old washer?"

"No problem. You still using this antique?" He gave a low whistle, not waiting for her answer. With a minimum of fuss, he hauled away her ancient washer.

She hurried to mop the spot the new appliances would occupy.

He returned in a few minutes with a second box. He stripped away the cardboard packaging and patted the dryer lovingly. "You're getting the best, ma'am. Yes, sirree, these here are top of the line."

With the same economy of motion he'd used in lugging away the old machine, he installed the new ones.

Jenny looked at the gleaming white appliances with panels resembling those of a spaceship. Or a computer. It didn't take much figuring to know who'd sent them.

"Thank you for all your trouble," she said.

"My pleasure, ma'am." With the tip of an imaginary hat, he left.

Jenny walked around the washer and dryer, fingering the array of buttons and knobs. David had bought the best. She tried to see the appliances for what they were—a gift. But her heart wasn't in the mood to accept gifts from a man who couldn't accept the only thing she could give him in return: her love.

A flash of anger surged through her. She welcomed it. Anger she understood. Anger she could deal with. How dare he think he could get away with it?

"Looks like we're moving up in the world," Mrs. Abernathy observed as she came into the kitchen.

"What . . . oh . . . these. David sent them. But he's got another thing coming if he thinks he can . . ."

"If thinks he can what?"

"Buy me off."

"You think that's what he's trying to do?"

"I know it is." She fanned her anger, the emotion feeling good after all these weeks of nothingness.

"David doesn't strike me as the kind to buy his way out of a relationship."

The mild rebuke in Mrs. Abernathy's voice had Jenny bristling. "You're siding with him?"

The old lady just smiled.

David swallowed a bite of baked apple his housekeeper had put before him and was immediately ferried back in time to when he and Jenny had picked apples together.

The morning had been laced with sunshine, laughter, and Jenny's special brand of magic. They'd picked enough apples for her to can three dozen jars of applesauce. The memory of the thick, chunky sauce had him licking his lips. Other memories tumbled head over heels upon it.

Why did his mind pick now to remember the way her eyes lit up when she was happy? The gentleness of her voice as she comforted a child? The sweetness of her smile when she looked at him? From there it was only a slight jump to think of the softness of her skin, the freckles that danced across her nose, the curve of her lips.

He pushed his plate away and stood. All this because of a baked apple. Heaven only knew what would happen if he were to actually see her again.

The image took shape before the thought was fully formed. He needed to see her, and then perhaps he could exorcise her from his mind. That was it. He'd prove to himself that what he was feeling was simple nostalgia for a place. Jenny had been no more than a pleasant diversion.

His fork fell from his fingers. He stalked to his den, which was off-limits to Mrs. Carson, the housekeeper, and pulled out the canvas he'd stored in a closet.

Jenny's face smiled back at him. A golden-haired child lay nestled in her arms. It was rough, certainly no masterpiece. He hadn't shown it to anyone. It was for his eyes alone. He turned his gaze away, not needing the picture to conjure up the image of Jenny's face.

Who was he trying to fool? He didn't want to exorcise her. And Jenny was no mere diversion. She'd worked her way into his heart and mind without even trying. So what *did* he want?

To be with her. For the rest of his life.

He returned to the dining room to find his housekeeper looking at him with more than her customary disapproval. "I'll be leaving tomorrow morning. I won't be coming back."

A harrumph was Mrs. Carson's only acknowledgment of his announcement.

He called his office manager, told her to hold down the fort, and that he'd be in touch. He grinned, feeling better than he had in weeks.

Only later, when he was packing, did doubts creep into his mind. What if Jenny refused to take him back? What about the wedding? Had she found someone else, someone who wasn't as thickheaded as he was? What if she'd discovered that she didn't love him after all? What if she'd forgotten?

He had one saving grace, one that Jenny herself had bestowed upon him. Jenny had said that she loved him. Jenny, who had enough love for all the lost, needy creatures of the world, loved him. If a person as wonderful as Jenny loved him, then he'd better have enough grit to *make* her see that they belonged together.

The following morning, he left an envelope for Mrs. Carson with a month's wages, a bonus, and a note of dismissal. He looked around, trying to find anything that he wanted to take with him. That he found nothing was final proof that he was making the right decision.

At the last minute, he dug some brown wrapping paper and tape from a closet. The package was bulky, awkward, and, he hoped, the key to his future.

The lilting sound of laughter reached him before he ever opened the gate to Jenny's yard. The greeting he'd planned died on his lips as he took in the sight before him.

A red kerchief around her eyes, Jenny staggered across the yard, calling out dire threats if someone didn't let her catch them. Trevor, Travis, and three other children dodged her as she stumbled around, arms outstretched. Ralph barked madly, running between Jenny's legs.

He should say something, tell her that he was here. His heart slammed against his chest, robbing him of words. A voice whispered inside his heart that there had always been only one woman and he had been waiting all his life for her.

He put a finger to his lips when the twins spotted him.

"Hey, where is everybody?" Jenny asked.

David planted himself in her path. The children's giggling silenced as she neared him.

"All right. Someone give me a break." Her hands found his shirt. "I got you!" She tore off the blindfold. "David!"

There was so much he wanted to say. But not now, not with an audience. "Right the first time."

Five pairs of eyes watched with avid interest as she unclutched the shirt and backed up a few steps.

"Hey, Jenny, David's back," Travis said unnecessarily.

"Go into the kitchen and ask Mrs. Abernathy to give you some cookies," Jenny said, her gaze never leaving David.

"We want to watch you and David kiss and make up." A wide grin split Trevor's face.

"Yeah," Travis backed him up.

The rest of the children giggled.

Jenny didn't raise her voice, but a thread of steel ran through it. "In the kitchen. Now."

"We never get to stick around for the good stuff," Travis muttered.

With obvious reluctance, they headed to the house.

"We were . . . uh . . . playing blindman's buff," she said once she and David were alone.

He stuffed his hands into his pockets to keep from touching her. "I figured that out."

"What're you doing here?"

How could he explain what he'd been through these past weeks? "I had to see you."

She managed a smile that trembled around the edges more than it curved. "Oh?"

Fear tightened around his heart. "Travis mentioned something about a wedding in his letter."

"That's right."

He grimaced. She was going to make him sweat. Not that he didn't deserve it. "Who's getting married?" The words almost choked him.

"Mrs. Abernathy and Mr. Ambrose. They've been courting for several weeks. They're getting married day after tomorrow."

His sigh of relief came out in a whoosh. "That sly old fox."

"Mr. Ambrose knows how to treat a lady," she said, a faint smile sliding across her lips.

"And you think I don't?" Unable to wait any longer, he closed the distance between them. Bodies pressing together, hearts beating as one, he kissed her with such burning intensity that they were both breathless when he finally released her.

She tilted her head to one side, considering. "Well, maybe you do know how to do some things."

Now that the matter of the wedding was cleared up,

he stumbled for what to say next. In desperation, he reverted to what he was familiar with. "How's the computer working out? Did you learn how to run the mailing list? What about—"

"David, did you come all this way to discuss business?"

He actually felt like squirming. "Not exactly."

"Why did you come?"

He stalled, looking at her eyes for a hint of what she felt. Had she stopped loving him? He wouldn't blame her if she had. He'd acted like a world-class jerk. "Don't you know?"

"You'll have to tell me."

He sighed. She wasn't going to make it easy for him. "I came because I heard the fairies."

"The fairies?"

"The ones you told me I'd hear if I only listened."

"You listened for them?"

He nodded, certain she'd say the three words he'd come all this way to hear.

"Why?" The one word was a challenge. He prayed he could meet it.

"Because of you."

"You listened for the fairies because of me? Why?" He heard the smile in her voice.

"Because I love you!"

There, he'd said it. The words he believed he'd never be able to say, much less mean, rushed from his lips. He pressed a kiss to her lips.

She melted into his embrace. The kiss kindled a spiral of pleasure deep within her. She slid her arms around him, letting the needs of the past few weeks take over. His mouth was warm and giving one minute, hot and demanding the next.

She answered the demand with equal hunger, hunger too long denied.

"You were right," he said when he lifted his head. "I was running away. It feels like I've been running forever. Until you. I love you," he said again.

Tears stung her eyes at the words she'd waited to hear, sweet tears that dampened her cheeks. Dreams really did come true. And knights in shining armor did exist.

"Jenny, are you crying?"

"I always cry when I'm this happy." Happy didn't describe how she felt. Ecstatic. Delirious.

"Does this mean you're going to cry at our wedding?"

Her thoughts scattered like sunbeams caught in the breeze. "Wedding?"

"The one we're going to have tomorrow."

"You're crazy." And she loved him for it.

"You mean you're going to make me wait?"

A bubble of laughter spilled over. "Just a week. As soon as Mrs. Abernathy and Mr. Ambrose are back from their honeymoon."

"A week," he agreed reluctantly. "But no longer."

"Maybe a little longer," she said, unable to resist teasing him. "We need to invite guests, order a cake, buy a dress—"

"You don't need a dress. You look great just like you are."

She glanced down at her frayed cutoffs and grubby T-shirt. "You really are crazy, you know that?"

"Yeah. About you." He fitted his finger under her

chin, tilting it up so that her eyes met his.

"I ought to be angry with you. About that bribe."

"Bribe?" His face was a picture of little-boy guilt.

She donned her fiercest look. "The washer and dryer."

"Washer and dryer?"

"The ones you had delivered."

"You knew it was me?"

She rolled her eyes in exasperation. And love. Always love. "Of course I knew."

"Oh."

He looked so sheepish that she smiled, a real, honest-to-goodness smile that stretched across her face.

"They weren't a bribe. Travis wrote me and said the washing machine died. I knew you needed a new one and knew you wouldn't accept a gift." He didn't give her a chance to deny the charge. "I have something for you." He handed her a large package and watched as she ripped away the paper.

She stared at the painting of herself and Katie.

He promised himself he wouldn't rush her; he'd wait for her reaction. When she continued to stare at it, he couldn't wait any longer. "Do you like it?"

"It's wonderful." She swallowed over the lump in her throat. "You never said you could paint like this."

"I never could . . . before. It took you to give me the courage. Happy?"

Love, sweet and so very right, filled her. "So much that I'm afraid to believe it's real."

"It's real, all right. I know I'm not a very good risk, but I'll do everything I can to make you happy."

"I know."

"You won't be sorry."

She put a finger to his lips. "How could I be? I have everything I ever wanted."

"I love you." The words that had refused to come in the past now slipped off his tongue with an ease that still managed to surprise him.

"And I love you."

They found the rest of the family gathered in the kitchen.

"It's about time," Mrs. Abernathy said when Jenny told them the news. She clapped David on the back. "I always knew you had it in you. When's the wedding?"

"As soon as you two get back from your honeymoon," David said, clasping Jenny's hand in his.

Love trickled through her at the possessiveness in his voice. Together, they'd make a family. There'd be children. Lots of them. Children of the heart.

"David, we'd like you to give the bride away," Mr. Ambrose said with grave dignity.

David looked at Mrs. Abernathy, who smiled widely. "Nothing would make us happier," she said.

"I'd be honored."

The wedding was beautiful in its simplicity. Trevor and Travis managed to seat the guests with only a minimum of giggling. Mr. Zwiebel served as best man.

The only hitch occurred when Ralph found the champagne David had ordered and knocked a bottle off the counter, lapping up its contents. He hiccupped through the ceremony.

David felt a knot form in his throat as he looked at Jenny, radiant in a dress the color of irises with flowers woven through her hair. Listening to the couple recite their vows, he pictured himself and Jenny repeating the same words. The image was so vivid that he was jolted back to reality only when the minister asked who gave the bride in marriage.

"I do," David said, his voice little more than a croak. He wondered how he got the words out at all. He tried again. "I do."

A wad of emotion clogged his throat as he watched the rest of the ceremony. His gaze caught Jenny's. And held. The love that shone in her eyes was as real a force as any other in nature. That he'd spent so much time denying it filled him with shame.

The minister completed the rites, finishing with, "You may now kiss the bride."

The newlyweds kissed to the cheers of the onlookers.

That evening, after seeing them off on a honeymoon to the Bahamas—David's treat—he and Jenny settled on the porch swing. He remembered another evening, when he'd given in to the impulse to kiss Jenny. Need pulsed through him now as he touched his lips to hers.

"Only another week," she said, her husky voice turning his insides to marshmallow.

"An eternity."

The night enfolded them, the stars sparkling like bangles against a sky of black velvet.

Her hand found his. "Listen."

He did as she bade and heard a soft, clear tune, like that of a flute. The breeze whispered an accompaniment.

"The fairies are happy for us," she whispered.

David had no trouble believing it at all.